THE
KAIJU
KID

Also by **Shane McKenzie**

THE
KAIJU
KID

SHANE
MCKENZIE

ERASERHEAD PRESS
PORTLAND, OREGON

ERASERHEAD PRESS
205 NE BRYANT
PORTLAND, OR 97211

WWW.ERASERHEADPRESS.COM

ISBN: 978-1-62105-278-4

FORTUNE CITY

It was a hot day in Fortune City. The citizens slogged through the streets, tongues hanging from mouths, flesh glistening with sweat. The concrete was like a frying pan, melting the rubber on tires and the bottoms of shoes.

So when they first felt the cool breeze blow in, they were grateful. Ecstatic really.

People stopped in their tracks, eyes closed as they allowed the chilled air to sweep over them. Drivers stepped out of their vehicles to feel the arctic caress of this mystery wind slap against their sweat-soaked skin. There was a smile on every face. A collective sigh of relief.

The sighs became screams when the giant bird cast its titanic shadow over the city, zooming over skyscrapers and highways. Its caw was like a clap of thunder, so deep and loud that glass shattered on buildings and cars alike. The bird's eyes shone a dark violet color, like two giant black light orbs. The talons on its leathery feet were as black as ink, as long as sedans.

"Condoria!" a woman screamed, clutching her child

7

to her chest and pointing toward the sky. "Oh jesus… Run!"

Others made similar exclamations, and just as the citizens began to scatter, race in all directions, the massive bird squeezed out an egg. It was orange, the size of a house, shining as bright as the sun. The egg smashed into a building, cracking on impact. A wave of molten lava exploded out of the shell, splashing against the building and melting it almost instantly. Bright orange magma rained down in the streets, along with liquefied metal and glass.

The woman with the child pressed to her chest shrieked once, loud and shrill, before she and her infant were enveloped in lava. Two red skeletons stood in their place, but only for a moment before the bones collapsed and blended in with the rushing magma. Drivers were fused to their vehicles by molten metal and rock, only having seconds to scream in agony before their flesh sloughed off their bones.

Condoria perched on top of the melting building, spread her bat-like wings. Her wingspan was nearly the size of the building she stood upon, an orange glow reflecting off the black, venous membranes of her wings. She screeched—more glass exploded, car alarms went off. She launched herself from the building, swooped over the street. Her wings cut buildings in half as she flew, burying terrified citizens in rubble. She opened her razor-sharp beak, scooped up a mouthful of humans. They screamed, flailing and fighting each other to get out, to jump to freedom even if it meant death. But she slammed her beak shut at the same time that her talons closed over more human flesh. Severed arms and legs, a few heads fell from her mouth, spraying blood as they dropped back to the broken concrete beneath. The few humans who had survived her clutching claws—and who were still in her grasp—exploded into hysterics, thrashing to free themselves, surrounded by dead men and woman who were impaled by the giant bird's talons.

She flapped her wings, hovered over the street, opened her beak. Entrails and tattered flesh and splintered bone littered her mouth, and she jammed one clawful of humans in, crunching them into a thick red paste. Then the other clawful. Blood and meat splashed to the street beneath her.

The ground began to rumble then. The cool breeze that had only moments before brought a smile to every face in the city became an icy storm that cut flesh like razor blades. The sky turned ashen as a heavy snow began to fall, coming out of nowhere, frosting the buildings and concrete in minutes.

A mighty roar rang out, coming from the direction that most of the citizens were running toward. They stopped, tried to turn tail, but Condoria was there waiting, dropped another egg that cracked in the street, sent a wave of molten lava toward them, incinerating the crowd.

One man driving an 18-wheeler climbed out of the cab, stood on the truck's trailer. The vehicle lowered more and more as the lava melted it down. His skin was red, spewing sweat. But the man wasn't paying attention to that anymore. His eyes were aimed toward the horizon where the strong gusts of freezing wind were coming from, hitting him so hard he was nearly thrown right off his truck.

The lava became a solid river of rock and metal, hissing and sizzling as the sudden winter cooled it almost instantly.

"It's…it's A-Avalanx!" He pointed a shaking finger as the giant stomped toward the city. Towering over their tallest building. The fog caused by the frosty winds and snow was so thick that only the behemoth's silhouette could be seen at first. Each step it took covered miles, shook the very earth. In mere moments, Avalanx appeared, giant icicles falling from his white fur and crashing to the street.

One icicle stabbed straight through an SUV, pinning it to the asphalt. The driver within must have been mid-scream when the frozen lance hit him, entering his mouth and stretching it wide like a snake with its jaw unhinged. The corners of his mouth split all the way down to his neck, spraying blood that froze instantly.

Avalanx roared, smashed a building to rubble with a swing of his massive arm. The stone and metal and glass slammed down on the street, turning fleeing bodies into flattened smears on the blacktop. The colossal beast opened its mouth, its eyes glowing a bright, arctic blue, and unleashed a beam of icy breath that froze the horde of panicked patrons, some falling over and shattering on the ground like ice sculptures. The snow and sleet fell heavier now, the winds became more violent.

Avalanx reached down with his massive hand, grabbed the human popsicles, breaking them into pieces as he clutched his fist, then tossed the frozen mush into his mouth. As he swallowed, he swung his arm again, totaling another building. Then another gust of wintery death breath and another mouthful of human flesh slush.

Condoria flew over the city, dropping eggs, unleashing the liquid hell, gorging on the hysterical humans who had nowhere to run, nowhere to hide.

Avalanx smashed buildings as easily as a child knocking over cardboard cutouts. Turning the once smoldering city into an icy wasteland.

The monsters ate and destroyed until they had their fill. Just like they always did.

By the time the military arrived to defend the city, the Kaiju were gone, leaving the streets covered in lava and ice and human remains.

"Jesus fucking Christ," one soldier said, then turned his head and vomited over a pile of bones. The air was still frosty, the snow still falling. The puke turned solid instantly.

"Avalanx," another soldier said, shaking his head and staring at the aftermath. "And Condoria it looks like."

"What's that?"

"The most fearsome fucking Kaiju in the world, man. Even if we made it on time, there wouldn't have been a fucking thing we could have done to stop them."

"I…I thought Tyranagon was the most fearsome."

The soldier picked up a frosted skull, ran his thumb over the frozen teeth. "He used to be. But he disappeared. That big fucker hasn't shown himself since the Eternal City incident."

"Eternal City. Those fucking giant fuckwads can't do shit to Eternal City."

"Yeah…well this ain't no fuckin' Eternal City, now is it?"

The soldiers shivered as they began searching for survivors, not expecting to find a single one.

A FUCKING
EMBARRASSMENT

"That was sick!" Gigataur said, pumping his clawed fists as Mom soared into their lair. "Did you bring us a taste? Come on...I'm starving."

"Mom, you were awesome," Zapstress said. She grinned wide as blue electric current rode her black, slick flesh. "That city never stood a chance."

Krick sat in the corner of their mountain cave, holding his knees to his chest. He had watched the action along with his brother and sister, but he couldn't find it as exciting as they did. Anytime his parents went out on destruction trips like that, the footage played automatically in the kids' minds, seeing through their parents eyes. Krick wanted to turn it off, but he couldn't. He had to watch as all those poor people were butchered, smashed and melted and frozen and chewed up. It made him sick. Sure, he'd eat the stuff. He had to if he wanted to live. But killing them was different. He wasn't sure if he could ever make himself do it, no matter how upset it made his parents. Especially his father.

Mom flapped her wings a few times, smiling wide as Gigataur and Zapstress showered her with admiration. Her long, scaly neck quivered as she gagged, then she opened her beak wide and let the pile of meat spill from her throat. Reds and pinks and purples and grays. White bone sticking out here and there. The mush steamed as Dad entered the cave. He patted his belly and picked his teeth.

"Go ahead, kids," Mom said, then stepped aside as Gigataur and Zapstress dug in, stuffing their faces, moaning as they gorged the freshly heaved meal.

She looked over at Krick who stayed in his place in the corner and watched his siblings feast. His stomach rumbled, but he knew better than to try and force his way in. He'd take whatever was left over, just like always. Would probably have to suck the marrow out of the bones again.

"He's a fucking embarrassment," Dad had said just the other night. "He doesn't fit in with the family, Connie. What are we supposed to do with a fucking monster who's too much of a pussy to destroy anything?"

Krick had pretended to be asleep, wiping the slimy tears as they poured from his only eye.

"He's our son, Aval. That's all that matters," Mom had said. "He'll come around. He's just…special. That's all. A late bloomer."

Gigataur slurped up a rope of purple intestine, licked his lips. Each of his four hands was digging into the bloody mound, taking turns stuffing sloppy balls of meat into his mouth, his giant fangs crushing bone with ease. He shot Krick a look, smirked, then belched and snickered.

Zapstress had her back to Krick, ignoring him as usual. She used her electricity to cook the meat before stuffing her face with it. Her eel-like body writhed as she feasted. The electric current crackled as it jumped from her skin and popped in the air.

Krick flinched when a ribbon of current burst just a few feet away from him, memories of his brother holding him down while his sister zapped him again and again flooding his mind.

"Krick, honey," Mom said. She tucked her wings and strolled across the cave. "Aren't you hungry?"

Krick shrugged, pulled his knees in tighter. It was always hard for him to look his mom and dad in the face after they had caused so much death and destruction.

"Let him starve," Dad said, sleet precipitating from his mouth as he spoke. "You want to eat, you need to fight for it. Survival of the fittest…or some shit like that. You hungry, boy? Get your fat ass up and take your share. You don't ask for it, you fucking take it!"

"Yeah, Krick. Come on over. I dare you," Gigataur said, spitting bone shards and blood from his red-painted mouth.

Zapstress just laughed as she whipped her tail, shooting a bolt of electricity at him. It hit him in the arm and he yelped and jumped to his feet.

"That hurt!" Krick said.

Zapstress looked over her shoulder at him, shook her head and smiled. The meat in her hands smoked as she cooked it, then pushed it past her long, pointy teeth.

Mom glared at Dad, hissing, standing tall and stretching her neck. Dad held her stare for a moment, but then snorted and looked away, staring out of their cave and into the distant mountain ranges that surrounded their home.

Mom opened her wings, flapped them hard and fast. Krick's brother and sister were lifted off their feet, thrown into the stone wall across the cave. They grunted, growled, then jumped back on their feet and faced their mother as if they were going to attack her. They quickly lowered their eyes and eventually escaped to their rooms.

"Go ahead, Krick. Eat up," Mom said, then leaned over and kissed him on the forehead, stroked his tiny, flightless wings.

Dad stretched out on the floor, rested his head on a pillow of snow. He yawned, smacked his mouth. Crystalized blood coated his lips, clung to his fur. He watched as Krick tiptoed toward the food, then snorted again and shook his head.

"Goddamn disgrace." Then he turned so his back was to Krick and Mom, and within seconds, was snoring. Each snore released a beam of icy breath that exploded out into the air, hitting mountain tops way off in the distance.

Krick plopped down beside what was left of his parents' kill. He absently grabbed a leg, mostly dissolved by Mom's stomach acids, and popped it into his mouth. The pruned flesh was stripped from the bone as he scraped his teeth across it and pulled it back out of his mouth. A tear escaped his eye, splashed on the cave floor and froze.

Mom sat beside him, wrapped one wing around him. "Don't put too much thought into it, sweetheart. But you know…your dad's right. We're monsters, baby. Monsters destroy. Kill. Without that, we're nothing. You understand that, don't you?"

Krick shrugged, poked at a woman's head with his finger. There was a bite taken out of her cranium, the brains spilling out. Krick scooped them out, sucked them up. Always his favorite.

"I don't know, Mom. I guess…I just don't get it. Why do we have to destroy cities all the time? And all those people…they never did anything to us. Why do we have to kill them like that?"

"To survive. Those people? You know what they eat? Smaller animals. Or bigger, stupider animals. That's just the way it is. Everything is food for something else. Except for us."

Krick thought back to all the training sessions he had had with his parents, side by side with Gigataur and Zapstress. His siblings were natural born Kaiju. Destroying was automatic for them. They had discovered their special abilities before they could even walk.

But not Krick. He would always hurt himself somehow, get laughed at by his brother and sister. His father used to beat him, thinking it would toughen him up, accelerate the learning process. But instead, it only made Krick cry, run to his mother for support.

Dad would make giant mock cities with his ice breath and Mom would fly around the mountains, collecting goats to act as fleeing people. Gigataur and Zapstress looked like they were having the time of their lives, smashing ice buildings, devouring handfuls of goats.

Krick, wanting so desperately to fit in and to impress his father, swung as hard as he could, smashing his fist into the nearest building. The ice didn't even budge. Krick's red knuckles split and bled, and he shrieked, fell to the ground bawling. The goats climbed his body and baaaahed, seeing him as no threat whatsoever.

"Well maybe I wasn't supposed to be a monster, Mom. Maybe it was a mistake. You know?" Krick scratched one of the black spots that covered his red, spongy body. They always itched, used to drive him crazy, but he was starting to get used to it.

"Of course you were supposed to be a monster. You're part of the most feared family of Kaiju in the world, don't you realize that? Your father and I...we're legends, baby. Parents tell stories about us to their children. People live in fear at all times, wondering if Condoria or Avalanx will come to their city. And one day, they will say the same about you and your brother and sister. You'll see."

"Yeah, Gigataur and Zapstress, but not me. They'll laugh at me. Their armies would kill me. It wouldn't even be hard. I don't have any special abilities...I'm just a useless pile of blubber." He scooped up the last of the masticated, semi-digested meat and filled his mouth, then wiped another tear from his giant eye.

"Krick," Mom said, holding him tighter, resting her beak on the top of his head. "You'll find your ability. It's in you. All Kaiju have at least one. We just have to find search for it. Dig deep."

"I've tried. I've tried so hard…but…but all I can do is this." Krick squeezed his fists, strained so hard that his body shook. One of the black spots on his belly bulged, looked like a zit ready to pop. A tiny version of Krick pushed itself out and floated down to the floor as it flapped its miniature wings. Its skin was a lighter shade of red, paler, diseased. Its eye was dark yellow, covered in pus that leaked down its face and into its mouth. It struggled to walk, dragging its feet, coughing and wheezing. Green phlegm sprayed from its mouth and splashed to the floor. It only made it a few steps before falling over. Dead.

Mom stared at the tiny version of her son, put on an obvious fake smile. "Hey…I've never seen an ability like that. It's…original at least, right?"

Krick rolled his eye, sighed. "Dad was so mad at me when I first did that…I could see how disgusted he was just to look at me. He hates me, doesn't he? Just like Gigataur and Zapstress. They all hate me."

"That's not true. We're family. We might be proud, but we love each other. We stick together."

"You're not ashamed of me, Mom? I can't…do anything." Krick never felt like he truly fit in. There were times he had thought about running away…or just jumping right off the mountain. He didn't think his family would even notice he was gone. Either that or they'd throw a party.

Mom kissed him again, yawned. "Stop talking like that, baby. You've got a big day tomorrow."

"What do you mean…tomorrow? What's happening tomorrow?"

She curled up next to Dad, wiggled her body as she settled in. "Come on, Krick. You know. It's what you and your brother and sister have been training for. It's your first day."

Oh my god…that's tomorrow? I'll be killed!

"Mom…no. I-I can't. You know I can't."

"Shhh. Quiet now, baby. I'm…exhausted. You'll do…just…fine. I know…you will…" And then she was asleep, leaving Krick alone with his thoughts.

Tomorrow. They're going to take the three of us to our first real city tomorrow. And they'll all laugh at me. Even Mom will be embarrassed to have me as a son when she sees me fail.

Krick snuck past his slumbering parents, stood right on the edge of the cliff. Below him was a seemingly endless abyss of ice and snow and rock. Strong winds threatened to push him over, and he contemplated just tipping himself forward, letting the wind take him away.

But his cowardice won, as it always did, and he went back to his corner, curled up, and dreaded being alive.

Pelican Bay. Krick thought it was a silly name. Didn't seem very intimidating, actually made him feel a little bit better about the situation.

"This should be a piece of cake," Dad said. "No messing around, though. Sometimes these little cities will surprise you. You remember Cyclopiton?"

Gigataur and Zapstress nodded, licking their lips as they stared at the city in the distance. Krick had never heard that name before.

"It was a city like this that did him in. Hidden missiles. Blew his fat head right off his shoulders."

Pelican Bay suddenly didn't sound so silly anymore.

Dad, Gigataur, and Zapstress waded through the ocean toward the city. Krick sat on Mom's shoulders as she soared over the water. Dad created a curtain of fog to hide them.

"One of you should be able to handle Pelican Bay… so the three of you should take it no problem. I want to see smashed buildings. I want to see people screaming, running in all directions, you got me? I want total destruction. Eat all you can, kids." He pulled Gigataur and Zapstress close, hugged them. "Make me proud."

Krick wanted so bad to be hugged by his father. He sighed from his mother's shoulders, crossed his arms. She turned her long neck so she could look back at him, smiled, rolled her eyes playfully. Then she pecked a kiss on his forehead before picking up speed and zooming toward the city. She was a great mother. The best mother a monster could ever ask for.

"Here we go, Krick. You can do this, I know you can."

Below them, Gigataur and Zapstress roared as they approached the coast.

It was time to put their training to the test.

PELICAN BAY

It was Fish Fest in Pelican Bay. The biggest festival of the year. Fish Fest was important to the small city because it brought in so many tourists, helped keep the city financially afloat for the rest of the year. The flounder were breeding. Folks could barely step into the water without stomping on one hiding in the sand. The beaches were covered with gig-pole-toting tourists, stabbing their spears into the sand and pulling out massive flounder one after another.

Rachel hated Fish Fest. She thought fish was gross and didn't understand how anyone ate it. Her mom took her to the beach, which she normally loved. Swimming and building castles and pretending like she was the princess who lived inside. But there were too many people during the stupid flounder festival, and she didn't have enough room to do much but dig a hole.

"Can we go home now?" Rachel said, tugging on the bottom of her mother's sun dress.

"Aren't you having fun?" her mother said. She didn't even bother to look up from the novel she was reading. "Look at all these kids, honey. Go make some friends."

"I don't want any friends. I'm a princess. I need my castle!"

"Well that's too bad." Her mother sipped on her margarita, licked the green slush from her lips. "Go entertain yourself. Mommy's busy."

Rachel growled and stomped her foot. She wished all these people would disappear. Just go away so she could play on the beach by herself.

I hate all of these people and I hate flounders and I hate everything!

"What the hell is that?" A male tourist dropped his gig pole and pointed up at the sky. A loud, ear-shattering screech filled the air like Gabriel's trumpet announcing the end of the world.

The fishermen paused, a few with flopping flounder impaled on the end of their spear. Children playing in the sand froze in place. All eyes were on the sky as the giant bird soared overhead.

"Mommy?" Rachel said, now clinging to her mother's leg.

Her mother's book had fallen into the sand. She held her margarita with shaking hands, the straw clinking against the edge of the glass. Her mouth opened and closed, but she was only making a squeaking sound.

"Fuck me! It's Condoria!" a man shrieked, then tossed his gig pole into the water and sprinted toward the parking lot.

But the bird never landed. Another monster dropped from its back and slammed down hard on the beach. Sand poofed up into the air, blocking Rachel from seeing the

24

thing too good. The sand cleared and everyone screamed. The monster was on its side, legs kicking, clutching its belly as if the fall had injured it. Its skin was as red as the devil, black spots covering its body like lesions.

As the beachgoers continued to scream and scramble over each other in search of safety, the massive beast flinched, sat up and faced them. It had one giant eye, as orange as pumpkin flesh. Thick arms hung at its sides, the legs short and stubby. The creature was hairless, looked flabby and smooth, almost soft as if it were covered in baby fat. It had tiny bat-like wings on its back that flapped uselessly.

Even as the people shrieked and ran for their lives, the monster just sat there, staring at them, almost as if it were scared of them instead of the other way around. It was such a curious site that a few of the people stopped running so they could study the beast.

"What's it doing?" one man said.

"Look at it, Mommy," Rachel said as she smiled and pointed up at the monster who was now getting to its feet. "He's not mean. He's cute!"

"Cute? It's…hideous. Let's go home before it gets hungry. I can't believe a Kaiju is right here in Pelican Bay. I never thought they would… Rachel, what are you doing? Get back here now!"

Rachel strode toward the monster, now giggling and waving at it. It turned and looked at her, blinked its one eye.

"I like him, Mommy! I want him! Can I keep him? I want him I want him I want him!" Rachel stopped just in front of the monster. She dug her toes in the sand and waved up at him, smiling.

The monster stared at her, then opened his mouth. Rachel gasped, took a step back. She kept her eyes on him as everyone around her screamed for her to run, that the monster was going to eat her. She didn't know why, but she didn't believe that. Not this monster.

"Rachel, get away from that thing!" Her mother grabbed her from behind, tried to pull her away, but Rachel ripped her hand out of her mother's grasp.

The monster still didn't move, still had its mouth open. It looked to be…smiling at her. Though its teeth were sharp, they were small, mostly gums showing.

"What's going on?" another man said. "Why's it just standing there like that? What kind of Kaiju is this thing?"

"Hi," Rachel said.

The monster lifted its giant hand, stared at its palm as if not sure what to do with it, then waved at Rachel.

"See, Mommy? He's nice. He likes me!"

"Well would you look at—"

A ball of bright blue electricity exploded out of nowhere and hit Rachel's mother, enveloping her completely. She shook in place, mouth and eyes opened as wide as they could go. Blood squirted from her tear ducts, from her nose, rushed from her mouth. Her eyes exploded as her skin began to blacken. It wasn't until her body ruptured and sprayed the people around her with boiling hot gore that they took up running again.

"M-Mommy?" Rachel's eyes widened as she stared at the sloppy chunks of meat that used to be her mother lying in the sand. She screamed as she dropped to her knees, grabbing as many pieces as she could carry. A doctor can fix her. He can put her back together if I get enough pieces.

The monster whined, stomped its feet. Rachel screamed again when it scooped her up into his huge red arms. She dropped the wet pieces of her mom. The monster held her tight, but not tight enough to harm her. Rachel stopped shrieking as she and the monster faced the water.

Salt water splashed as the sea parted, and a giant form rolled out of the water toward the shore. It spun like a gargantuan bowling ball, covered in spikes twice the size of grown men. It hit the beach and threw sand in all directions, picking up speed. The thing was coming right at them, and the red monster turned his back to it, curled into a protective ball and surrounded Rachel with its soft body.

Rachel couldn't see, but she knew the giant spiked ball hit the red monster when he squealed in pain. There was a hard collision, and then weightlessness. They spun for a few moments, felt like they were floating away, and then a hard slam. Rachel's teeth clicked hard as she bounced around, and there was a sudden pain in her leg. The red monster uncurled itself once they finally settled, and Rachel saw that they were not on the beach anymore, but in the middle of the city. There was a huge chunk missing from the building next to them, pieces of it still falling off. The red monster sat up and groaned, glanced at her with his enormous eye, almost like he was embarrassed.

A few of the black spots on his skin started to pulsate. Rachel screamed when the small monsters crawled out and floated through the air, tiny wings flapping. They made gurgling sounds like they had the flu or something, but before they could land, more pieces of the building detached and crushed the smaller monsters against the street below. Green slime burst from their flattened bodies.

Rachel wept, wiping tears from her eyes and calling for her mother.

The red monster gasped, hopped back to his feet as he grabbed Rachel again and held her close. The spiky ball starting rolling again, making the ground shake as it came. The running people screamed as they were rolled over, pressed flat against the sand, ground into the tiny grains, shredding their flesh. Bodies hung from the spikes, blood and organs splattering in all directions as the monster spun forward and the bodies were torn apart.

Another form burst from the ocean, its body long and slick just like an eel's, the mouth full of long, pointy teeth. Blue lightning crackled as it rode this creature's wet hide and shot out of its body. Humans were cooked on contact. The monster ran on four legs, its six snake-like arms scooping up the barbequed remains of its victims and stuffing the black, charred flesh into its mouth. Dark blood and hot grease sprayed from its jaws as it chewed.

The barbed wrecking ball tore a hole right through the city. It broke the highway into pieces and smashed bridges. Countless people and vehicles were flattened and impaled. The monster left a trail of blood-soaked wreckage in its wake as it thundered forward. It finally came to rest in the center of the small cluster of buildings. Tattered bodies hung from its spikes, raining blood and minced entrails over the cracked concrete.

The ball shook, rattling against the concrete, then slowly opened. The monster roared as it burst open. Gore was flung in every direction, slapping against the buildings and slowly sliding down the sides.

Rachel clung to the spongy flesh of the red monster. She chewed on the inside of her cheek to keep from screaming or crying out and alerting the other more fierce monsters. Panicked voices filled the air as the tourists and residents alike scattered. They ran aimlessly; others jumped into their vehicles, all desperately trying to escape from the vicious creatures turning the city into their hellish playground.

The spiked monster stretched its four thick, armored arms, each equipped with long, curved claws. Its massive legs resembled an elephant's, the skin tough-looking and gray. When it roared again, it revealed the rows and rows of teeth, dripping with saliva.

"Don't let them get me," Rachel whispered as tears streamed down her chubby, freckled cheeks.

The red monster whined and turned its head from left to right. When it took off running, its feet leaving craters in the street, the people scattered and shrieked up at them.

"Get the fuck away from us!" a man screamed as he pulled his family behind him. He reached a brown minivan, and just as he placed his hand to the door handle, a burst of bright current engulfed the vehicle and blackened the metal instantly. The man froze, his body seizing, shaking violently as the voltage entered his flesh, rode into his wife, and then into their two children. They stood in place, hand in hand—cooking. Their flesh smoked and popped as it darkened.

The earth quaked as the electric eel beast charged. It slammed its jaws shut over the family and chewed them all together until they were nothing more than shredded meat and bone shards.

"Nonononono!" Rachel covered her ears and shook her head.

The red monster backed away from the eel, then spun and sprinted in the other direction. It lost its balance, stumbled and slammed its side into a building. Stone and metal rained over the street, but the building held, looked sturdier and stronger than the others. The bits of rubble that had broken free smashed down around the monster's feet, mangling a group of Asian men and women snapping pictures.

The red monster grunted, then dropped to a knee and placed Rachel on the ground. The pavement was sticky with blood. Body parts lay all around her. She shook her head and glared up at the monster, not sure what he was doing.

The monster reached out and nudged her with his knuckle, shoving her toward the double doors of the building. There was already a huge group of people inside, all huddled together and crying, mumbling to one another.

"Take me with you. You can't leave me here!"

The monster rubbed the back of his head and whined some more. The pupil in his massive eye darted around, looked anywhere but at Rachel.

"Please!"

The building started to shake, more glass and rock and metal falling all around them. Rachel screamed and ran to the monster who immediately scooped her into his hand and backed away from the building.

The spiked monster had its four arms wrapped around the building. Its teeth were bared as its claws tore into the structure like it was made from Play Doh. The bigger, scarier monster turned its head and stared right at Rachel, then growled as it peered into the red monster's eye. It roared, ripped the building from the ground with ease. Bodies spilled from the bottom like beans from an open can, splattering against the pavement below. An avalanche of rubble slammed into the congregation of people who had been inside of the building. Blood splashed out, some of it spraying Rachel in the face and stinging her eyes.

"Gghhaaaa!"

The beast shook the building, emptying it of its fleshy morsels, then swung it like a bat at the neighboring building, smashing both to rubble. It reached down, grabbed two handfuls of kicking and screaming human flesh, filled its mouth and swallowed.

The red monster growled, deep and guttural. Rachel realized the sound had come from his stomach just as he bent down and filled his fists with leaking corpses.

"Wh-what are you doing?"

Electricity shot through the air, crackled as it entered flesh and metal all around them. The entire city glowed blue as the eel creature pumped more and more voltage into it. People were cooked, and then consumed in bunches. Dark blood and melted fat coated the streets.

The red monster's pupil rolled until it was aimed at Rachel, then he swung her around and put her behind his back. But she could still hear the sound of him chewing, the bones crunching as he ate. Rachel thrashed and punched at the monster's hand, trying to free herself. She didn't know where she'd go or what she'd do, but she wanted to get away from the monsters. All of them. As far away as she could.

He's not nice. He's just like the others!

I want my mommy!

Rachel was able to spin herself around, then wiggle free from the hand. She stood on the thumb, but it was still too high to jump. When she saw that the spiked beast was just in front of her, chewing, she stuffed herself back into the fist, then peered out through the space between fingers.

The creature tilted its head back and swallowed, then opened its jaws and roared. It dropped down to its hands and feet, then curled itself back into a wrecking ball. The spikes aligning its body shot free from its shell, penetrated buildings and pavement and bodies. What remained of the city was turned to ruins as the monster rolled again, its body now almost entirely covered in the blood of thousands upon thousands of humans. When it uncurled, it lowered its face to the streets and gorged on the mutilated remains.

The red monster swung his arm back around so that it could look down at Rachel again. His mouth was dripping with gore. All Rachel could do was cry and pray to God to save her. The monster's eye squinted, and he whined again as he glared at her in his palm.

The two ferocious monsters filled their bellies, satiated their need for destruction, and then retreated back to the ocean where they seemed to disappear behind a white, winter-like fog.

The red monster watched them go, flapped its tiny wings as if expecting to fly away. The giant bird appeared out of the sky, swept down, gripped the red monster with its talons, and then soared into the air.

"No! No, let me go!" Rachel dropped to all fours and bit down hard on the monster's hand. Orange blood filled her mouth just as the fingers opened.

She realized how stupid she was once the wind whipped over her and she began plummeting toward the ground. Her mind was focused on getting away from the monsters, and now as she dropped, faster and faster, she screamed for the red monster to save her.

Its pupil swung toward her and its mouth unhinged as if screaming.

Rachel's body twisted in the air, and the last thing she saw was the blood-stained pavement below speeding toward her.

NO SON OF MINE

Krick and his mother arrived to the cave first, and he immediately ran to his corner, covered his face so he didn't have to look his mother in the eye.

"Krick…" she started, but didn't say another word.

She's embarrassed. Just like I knew she'd be. And I don't blame her.

"Just leave me alone!" He couldn't get that little girl's face out of his head. The way she had smiled at him, trusted him to keep her safe. It was like they had a connection, a friendship—child and monster. A connection he never felt with his own family. And now the little girl is nothing but a splatter of blood, bone, and entrails mixed in with the rest of the massacre they had left behind.

Gigataur and Zapstress entered the cave, cheering and cackling. Their faces and bodies were caked with gore, and they took one look at Krick balled up in his corner, and their laughter grew in intensity.

"What happened, Krick?" Gigataur said, picking bones from between his teeth. "Did all those scary little people frighten you, tough guy?"

Zapstress shook the blood from her face and head. "What the hell were you doing back there, little brother? Carrying that baby human around like she was your girlfriend or something. That it, Krick? You falling in love with the food now?"

"Shut up!" Krick roared, spittle flying from his lips. "Just…just shut up. Please…"

Gigataur puffed up his chest, started toward Krick. "Why don't you make me, blubber boy?"

"Enough," Mom said. "Just leave him be, will you?"

"No," Zapstress said. "I'm sick of him shaming our family. And now the people saw it too? They weren't even scared of him. No…I can't have them thinking our family is weak because of him. I say we kill him. Just end it now. I'll make it quick." Sparks ignited across her body, boiling the blood that still coated her, filling the cave with its meaty scent.

"You won't touch him," Mom said, spreading her wings. "Neither one of you. It was his first time out… give him a break."

"It was our first time out, too," Gigataur said, glaring at Krick over Mom's shoulder. "And we kicked ass. Did you see us? We wrecked that place. You ask me, looked more like he was trying to save the city rather than destroy it."

"I ate people too!" Krick shouted, returning his brother's stare, but still staying safely behind his mother. "I ate lots of people."

"Yeah," Zapstress said. "I saw you. Picking up the scraps. Those were our kills, not yours. Don't you have any dignity? You're like a goddamn scavenger."

"I am not!"

"Yes you are." Dad stepped into the cave, his expression austere. "You're not a monster. The offspring of Avalanx and Condoria should be feared by every living creature on this planet. Yet a little girl smiles at you... and you carry her around like your own personal pet human? You try and save her? A human child? My own son...my own fucking flesh and blood!"

"Aval—"

"Quiet! I've had enough of you protecting him. We are monsters. Kaiju. We aren't supposed to need protection. We're not supposed to hide behind our mothers and shiver."

"Dad...I'm sorry. I tried...I really tried." Krick couldn't hold back his tears, his words coming out sloppy and wet. "Please. Let me try again. I'll do b-better."

Gigataur and Zapstress snickered.

"You've already shown me what you can do. Your special ability seems to be bringing shame to your family. And I'm done with you." Dad's eyes shone blue, and he opened his mouth as if he were ready to blast Krick with his icy breath.

Mom screeched, flapped her wings as hard as she could. Dad didn't budge, but he closed his mouth, bared his teeth. Sleet burst from between his lips with every breath he took and piled up at his feet.

"I don't care what you say. He's my son...our son. We don't just discard our children. We might be monsters...but we're not fucking heartless. Aval...please.

Think about this."

"I've already thought it over. It's been a long time coming, Connie. And you know it. If you weren't here…I'd eat him myself. I'd rip him to pieces and let his brother and sister strip the meat off his bones."

Mom backed up until her body was pressed up against Krick. Krick could barely see through his tears now, the entire cave blurry. He bawled as his father expressed his hate for him. Not that it was a big surprise, but to hear the words said out loud, to confirm what he had always suspected cut like talons.

Dad snorted, the glow in his eyes diminishing. "He can stay the night here. But this cave is for family. And he's no son of mine. Not anymore. Tomorrow, he's gone." He slammed his fist against the cave wall, shaking it. It felt like it would crumble in on them. Then Dad turned his back to them, just like he always did to Krick, and stared off into the mountains.

"Thank God," Zapstress said. "It's about time."

"Bye bye, dog dick. The next time I see you…I'll bite your face off." Gigataur chuckled as he headed to his room, patting his meat-filled belly.

Mom stayed in front of Krick, shielding him. But she wouldn't look at him. Didn't say another word. She settled in, folded her wings, and laid her head down. Heat radiated off her body, making Krick comfortable and sleepy. He wanted so desperately to hug her, envelope himself in her feathers like he used to. But he didn't dare. He just sat there, rested his head against the wall. Sleep wouldn't come, so he contemplated what was in

38

store for him tomorrow.

Maybe I'll finally do it. I'll just jump off the mountain and let the wind take me away.

HOW TO BE A REAL MONSTER

When Krick opened his eye, the wind whipped his body from all directions. He hadn't even realized that he had fallen asleep.

Dad threw me out of the cave while I was sleeping. I'll be dead any second now.

As the thought flowed through his mind, he wasn't even upset. It was comforting somehow. It was finally over. His family could be happy, didn't have to worry about him bringing shame and embarrassment to them.

But he wasn't alone.

Talons dug into his shoulders, dimpling the spongy flesh to the point of hurting. Mom held him, flapping her wings, soaring high over the mountains.

Krick didn't recognize these mountains, had no idea where they were. The mountains here were black, steam rising from their peaks. The heat was intense, hotter than he had ever experienced in his life. And yet…it was comfortable. Like he belonged here. A nice change from their frozen cave.

"M-mom? What's going on?"

Then it struck him. She's going to kill me. She brought me here to drop me into one of these fire mountains... maybe to make Dad happy.

"It's time you learned, Krick. It's now or never."

"Please, Mom. Please don't kill me...I'll do better. I'll even run away. You won't ever have to see me again. None of you will!"

She actually laughed, shook her head. And then finally looked at him.

Krick didn't see animosity in her eyes. No hate. It was the look of a loving mother. The look she had always given him, no matter how many times he failed.

"I'm not going to kill you, sweetheart. I'm rescuing you. Well...kind of."

"Kind of? But...you said... You said it's time for me to learn. Will you please tell me what's going on here?" Another blast of heat hit him in the face. "Where are we? It's hot as hell out here."

"I think it's time you met someone. Someone who I think can help us."

"Who?"

"My dad. Your grandfather. He's been hiding for years...ever since the incident at Eternal City."

"Eternal City? You mean the indestructible city? The place with the giant Hero?"

"Yes. Your grandfather...he—"

"Tyranogon? Is it? Tell me, Mom, is my grandfather Tyranogon?" Even Krick had been impressed with the stories he had heard. Tyranogon was every young monster's hero. Krick had no desire to destroy or kill, but he still couldn't help but look up to him. He was a legend among monsters and humans alike.

His mom chuckled, nodded her head.

And he's my grandfather!

"Mom...why didn't you tell me? Do Gigataur or Zapstress know?"

They continued to fly, his mother now coasting, riding the hellish wind currents.

"No. Your father...he didn't want any of you to know. Pride, that's all. He wanted you all to look up to him, not your grandfather."

Krick smiled. "So I'm the only one who knows..."

He took pride in that. There wasn't much for him to be proud of, and he had never had anything that his siblings wanted. He'd always been the jealous one. But if they knew about this...

"He's here? Grandpa has been hiding in these fire mountains all this time?"

"Don't call him Grandpa. He'll kill you." She sort of giggled, rolling her eyes as if reliving some distant memory.

Then she went expressionless. "Seriously...he'll kill you. And these are called volcanoes, sweetheart. He's hiding inside one of them...I just can't remember... There!"

She changed directions so sharply that Krick shrieked, reached up and grabbed hold of the feathers on her belly.

They swooped toward the biggest volcano Krick had seen yet, at least twice as big as the mountain where their cave lay. Splashes of lava shot out the top, spraying the neighboring mountains, the glowing orange magma rolling down the volcano's side.

"How can he live inside of there and still be alive? Wouldn't he…I don't know, be melted or something?"

"Honestly, I haven't seen my dad since before you and your brother and sister were born. For all I know, he could be dead." She laughed again. "But if I know Tyranogon like I think I do, he's still alive. Way too stubborn to die."

She landed at the top of the volcano just as another small eruption shook the earth. The lava exploded out, sprayed Mom and Krick, but neither was fazed.

"We've got his blood in us. The heat can't hurt us, baby. Don't worry. Dad's a firebreather. The last fire-breather as far as anyone knows."

Krick giggled as the lava coated his body, sliding off his red skin like mercury. He leaned over, peered into the volcanoes peak.

Two massive black eyes stared right back at him. A growl erupted out along with another splash of lava, and then the mountain began to quake.

Krick jumped back, clutched his mother's belly, buried his face in her breast feathers.

"Daddy? It's Connie. You in there?"

The ground shook so hard and violently that Krick's mother flapped her wings, hovered over it. Another massive eruption blasted into the air, followed by two giant black hands. They gripped the lip of the volcanoes peak, crushing rock like it was moist bread.

The head appeared next, bigger than Krick's entire body, covered in dark scales with horns and spikes protruding out in vicious curves. The black eyes landed on Krick and his mother, squinted, then suddenly widened. The jaw unhinged, revealing a mouthful of long, sharp teeth, as yellow as fire. Twin balls of flame shot from the nostrils.

Krick cringed, expected to be eaten whole along with his mother.

It's been too long, he wanted to shout to her. He doesn't know who you are anymore! And we're going to die!

But instead of a monstrous roar, the sound that came out of the legendary beast's mouth was more like a squeal.

"Connie!" Tyranogon pulled the rest of his colossal body out of the volcano, hardly able to fit through with his bulbous belly. His wings uncurled, long and black, though there were rips along the membranes. The veins were fat, bulging, and misshapen. Though his grandfather was clearly overweight, it didn't take away from his fearsome presence. His skin shone in the orange glow of the lava, covered in thick black scales like crags of charred rock. A long, purple forked tongue shot out from between his lips every few seconds, covered in thick white mucus. Steam rolled from his mouth constantly.

"Daddy!" Condoria zoomed toward her father, wrapping her wings around his neck, nuzzling him.

Tyranogon wept as he covered her with fiery kisses, rubbing his cheek against hers.

Krick just hung there in his mother's talons, watching

as the two winged Kaiju embraced after years and years of being apart. Then one of Tyranogon's black eyes landed on Krick, and a massive, toothy grin spread across his face.

"You brought me something to eat? You shouldn't have, baby." He spit an inferno from between his scaly lips, enveloping Krick completely. When Krick still hung there, uncooked and unharmed, the old Kaiju squinted at him. "What the hell is that thing? Why doesn't it die?"

Krick's mom laughed, tossed Krick into the air so that he landed on her back. "This is my son, Daddy. Your grandson. Krick."

"My grandson? I...I have a grandson?"

Krick waved. "H-hi...Tyranogon."

"You sure he's yours, Connie? He's not as impressive as I'd always imagined your offspring would be. You still with that giant snow ape?"

"Dad...come on. Be nice."

"Well didn't I tell you all your kids would look like mutant monkeys?" Tyranogon shot fire from his nostrils as he sighed, then looked Krick over again. "Sorry about that. I didn't mean to offend."

Krick just shrugged, put on a fake smile. "Um... it's okay."

The legendary monster wasn't coming off as very legendary to Krick. He had expected for his very life to be in danger in Tyranogon's presence. That the Kaiju would be more out of control, more violent than this. The fat, gargantuan beast in front of him just seemed lonely, sad. Krick could tell by the look on his mother's face that she felt the same way.

Tyranogon clapped his giant hands together, making a sound like thunder. "You guys hungry? There's villages all around these mountains. No cities though. But the people…oh man. The people around here are delicious. Kind of spicy and sweet at the same time. You have to try them."

He stood at the top of the mountain, stretched his wings as far as they'd go. His wingspan was impressive, and Krick could only stare in awe as they began to flap. Then Tyranogon sort of winced, held his side, and folded the wings back down.

"Maybe later, okay? I'm a little stiff right now." He gasped as if he was out of breath. It looked like the simple act of flapping his wings took it out of him.

Is he out of shape? Krick thought.

Tyranogon didn't look so good, spitting sheets of fire as he panted.

"It's okay, Dad. I can't stay long anyway," Krick's mom said.

"What are you talking about? You just got here! You can't go…why would you even show up if you were going to rush off like that? Connie…please. Stay a while. I miss you." Smoke started to billow from his eyes. "I've been out here all alone for…God I don't even know."

"Well…can't you just leave this place? Come back with the rest of us?" Krick didn't mean to say it out loud. His mom shot him a quick look that told him to shut his mouth, but his grandfather was already glaring at him. "I mean…everyone still talks about you. They're still scared of you. It would be so cool to get to see you in action, that's all."

Tyranogon shook his head. "I wish it was that simple. The giant Hero…he…he beat me. He beat me in front of everyone. I could never evoke fear in the humans again…not after that."

"I love you, Dad. It really is great to see you," Krick's mom said, reaching behind her with her beak and grabbing hold of Krick by the fat on the back of his neck.

"Connie, don't go. I didn't even get a chance to spend time with my grandson."

She placed Krick into the palm of Tyranogon's hand. The giant beast lowered his head and stared at him, his hand shaking, scaly brow furrowed.

"You'll have plenty of time with him now, Dad. I'm leaving him with you."

"What?" Krick and Tyranogon said at the same time, both with their eyes glued to Condoria who was already flapping her wings to make a retreat.

"Mom," Krick said, hands pressed together as if praying. "Don't leave me here. Please."

"You'd rather I take you back to your father? So he can kill you? Eat you?"

"He was upset. He won't—"

"Yes he will. He wouldn't even hesitate, sweetheart. Monsters…especially men," she said and locked eyes with her father, "are very stubborn and proud beasts. They will eat their own young. They will run away from their families and go into hiding at the very idea of being ridiculed or embarrassed."

"Are you punishing me for leaving, Connie? You

have to understand…I had to—"

"I know that, Dad. I know. And I don't blame you. No…this is no punishment. I'm trying to save my child's life. That's all. He might be a red little monkey creature, but I love him."

Krick did his best not to get offended by her words. He knew she was only doing what she thought was best for him. One way or another, Krick couldn't help but imagine he was a dead monster.

"Teach him, Dad. Teach him to be a real monster. The kind of monster you used to be."

"Used to be?" Tyranogon clenched his fists, and Krick jumped out of his palm just in time before being smashed to mush. He clung to one of the horns sticking out of his grandfather's forearm.

Tyranogon stood up straighter, flexed his wings again, shot a massive wave of flame from his mouth. "I am Tyranogon! The most…the most feared…" The old Kaiju started panting again, had to sit down, and grabbed his side. His belly jiggled when he sat, and he hung his head.

"Avalanx wants to kill him. Krick…he just hasn't found himself yet."

Tyranogon plucked Krick off his arm, held him up in front of his eyes. "What's his special ability?"

Krick wasn't sure if it was the mounting fear boiling inside of him, or just some kind of automatic reaction, but a miniature minion popped free from one of his spots just then, fluttered down, coughing and hacking all the while. By the time it hit the side of the volcano, it was dead, now cooking on the hot rock.

Tyranogon watched it the whole way as it floated down and flapped its tiny wings. Then he shot Condoria another look, shook his head.

"I'll be back soon. We don't have much time. Avalanx will figure it out sooner or later. We need to show him that Krick can destroy and kill just as good as his brother and sister…even better than them. And you're the only one who can show him how, Dad. I love you both."

And then she flapped her wings and was gone.

Krick still dangled from his grandfather's claws, not sure what to say. When Tyranogon's eyes moved from the sky back to Krick, the lonely, tame beast he had been only moments before was gone. He looked ready to bite Krick in half, as if this was all Krick's idea.

"I'm…I'm so sorry. She didn't tell me she was bringing me here."

A ball of flame exploded into Krick's face then, and he stopped talking at once, lowered his eye so as not to meet his grandfather's gaze.

"So you disgraced your family? Father would rather kill you then let you embarrass him?" His voice was like a growl now, lava spilling out from between his teeth. "I don't blame him. Look at you. You're pathetic. Maybe I should just kill you now, make it easy on everyone."

Krick clenched his fists. More of the sick creatures popped out of his spots, fluttered down. "Go ahead. Kill me. Just do it already. I'm sick of everyone talking about it and doing nothing. You want to kill me? Then fucking kill me!"

Tyranogon actually flinched, steam billowing from his mouth and nostrils. "Not worth my time." He tossed Krick away like he was nothing more than a booger, sent him crashing into the neighboring volcano, then hurtling down the steep side until slamming into a massive rock. Ash coated his body and he was covered in scrapes and gouges. He peeked around the rock toward his grandfather who was already retreating back into his volcano.

I don't belong anywhere. What is wrong with me?

Krick remained in that spot the rest of the day. Didn't dare move, didn't dare make a sound. He hoped Tyranogon would change his mind, come crawling back out of his volcano to apologize and tell Krick that he would train him, show him how to be a real monster.

But the giant Kaiju never showed. When the day turned to night, Krick lay on his side, still resting up against the rock, and let sleep take him.

For the second time, Krick woke up in mid-air. His grandfather flew close to the ground, as if flying any higher was too much of a strain on him. He grunted with every flap of his wings and mumbled something under his breath about being the fiercest Kaiju in the world, but Krick didn't hear all of it over the rushing wind.

"W-where are we going!" Krick shrieked, clutching the scales on Tyranogon's toes.

"Ah, you're...awake. Good."

In the distance, what appeared to be a small village came into view. People began running when they saw the great beast flying toward them, retreating into their huts or their treetop homes. These people didn't wear clothes like the ones Krick had seen, and there weren't any cars or buildings or concrete around.

"Can you please t-tell me what's going on?"

"You're gonna go down there, and you're gonna… you're gonna kill those people. You're gonna kill them and eat them, just like a monster is supposed to." Tyranogon panted, his forked tongue just hanging from his mouth now.

"I-I can't. I can't kill them."

"It's you or them, monkey boy. Because if you don't, you're my…lunch. And I'm getting…hungry."

Then the claws pinching Krick's back released, and he went flying toward the village.

THE
VILLAGE
OF FIRE

The chief didn't understand why the fire god was punishing them. He and his people had prayed to Him, offered Him sacrifices. The fire god had grown fat on their enemies' flesh, burning their villages to ashes. It was believed that they had pleased Him, that He would reward them.

The fire god roared once and spat fire into the air. It looked like His belly had grown even more since the last time they had seen Him, jiggling as the wind hit it.

He clutched something in His hand. Some kind of red demon, and just as the chief were sure the fire god would wash their village with flame, He dropped the demon and flapped His wings hard, missing their huts by mere feet. It looked difficult for the fire god to lift Himself, barely missing the tops of the trees as He flew away.

The people slowly poked their heads out, exchanged glances with one another and began chattering, each of them wondering what they could have done to anger the fire god. Wondering what this hideous creature could be.

The chief sensed the panic. He threw his hands in the air and called for his tribe to face him, to listen. "May the fire above rain down upon me!"

"May the fire above rain down upon us all!" the men and women chanted back.

The chief—an ancient man, but who still towered over the other men, his shoulders wide and strong—stood on his charred tree stump, slammed the butt of his staff onto the scorched wood. "The fire god burns for us. There is no reason to believe we have angered Him. If that were so, our village would be blazing. Perhaps," the chief said as he spun to face the red demon, "our fire god sent us this creature as an offering. A protector! Our protector!"

The great red beast lay on its belly, face buried in the dirt. A deep trench was dug into the ground where the demon had landed and slid across the forest floor. The skin was as red as blood with black spots decorating its hide like a leopard's.

The chief called his men forward, ordered the women and children to stay inside. The men surrounded the chief, and he waved them in closer, spoke in a hushed tone.

"Perhaps this is another test. He is testing our strength. Our fierceness. Be ready."

The men all nodded and grunted their approval, their spears and bows at the ready. The chief stepped forward, wearing a deep scowl as he trudged toward the giant demon.

The demon didn't move. The chief signaled for his

people to stand back. As he grew nearer, he could feel the heat emanating off the beast. Sweat began to pour out of his skin.

Some of his men begged him to get away. Begged him to let them check it out first, but the chief insisted. He knew he must remain strong, not just in front of his tribe, but in the presence of the fire god. When he was just beside the demon, he let his palm hover over its red flesh. He prodded the beast in the back with his staff.

When the demon stirred, the men gasped. Even the chief retreated, but only a few steps before puffing out his chest and standing tall again.

A deep groan spilled from the creature's mouth as it sat up, rubbed its face with its massive hands. The demon had one giant eye the color of fire. It slowly rose to its feet, its eye glued to the men. The chief thought he sensed fear there. The demon seemed confused, lost. It could have easily crushed them if it wanted to, but it only stood there, its eye bouncing from man to man.

Then it opened its mouth. The chief thought that maybe the demon was trying to communicate with them, but before it had a chance, one of the men panicked, threw his spear with a shriek.

The spear hit the beast, stuck into one of its legs. Orange blood flowed and the demon roared, fell backward on its rear and yanked the spear out, then rocked back and forth as it pressed its hand to the wound.

The other men wasted no time. They sprinted forward. The chief tried to call them back but none would listen. If this beast was indeed a gift from the fire god, then they would all burn for their betrayal. Spears and arrows penetrated the monster's flesh, each one making it scream and roar, shaking the trees around them.

As the monster wept, hiding its face from the men, something on its skin began to move. The black spots on its hide began to pulsate, as if each one had its own beating heart. Something began to push against the black flesh from the inside, like a baby kicking from within its mother's womb.

The men gasped, began to back away. The monster continued to hide its face, continued to weep.

Tiny creatures crawled out of the spots. They resembled the giant monster, only they were about the size of the men. They rolled out, plopped to the dirt. Coughing, phlegm rattling at the back of their throats as they tried to breathe. Their skin was a sickly pink color, green mucus coating their eyes, dripping down their faces.

More and more of them kept coming, falling out of the demon's skin. The demon seemed oblivious to this, refusing to look at the men who had just attacked it. As more orange blood pumped from its wounds, more and more of the smaller creatures were birthed from its hide.

And when the smaller creatures saw the men, they moaned, flapped their tiny wings and came for them. The men tried to run, retreat back into their huts or their tree houses where their families waited, where they could guard them from the monsters now swarming their village.

One of the creatures stumbled into the nearest hut, hovering just above the ground. The chief ran toward it, his staff held over his head. He lost his footing and slammed face-first into the dirt, and could only watch as the demon fluttered toward the entrance. The woman and children screamed and hid behind the man of the family, held each other as the creature entered. It coughed, looked ready to fall over and die at any moment.

The man lunged forward, plunged the tip of his spear into the monster's eye, popping it like a ripe plumb. Thick, green jelly exploded from the wound, soaked the man from head to foot.

The monster groaned, clawing at the spear jutting from its face. A stream of hot green bile rocketed from its mouth, splashed across the woman and her two children.

The family shrieked, running around in circles, doing their best to clean the fluid off of each other. It smelled like rotting animal flesh and seemed to burn like acid.

By the time the creature had finally died, the family was no longer panicking. They stumbled out of their hut, all coughing, all wheezing. Most of the other huts and tree houses were already under attack by the creatures, but the hut nearest them was not. As a group, they stumbled inside, vomited over the family within.

The chief rose to his feet and called out to them, begged them to stop, but they ignored him. "Enough! Enough!"

The verdant bile sizzled over the family's flesh, soaked in. Within minutes, they were on their feet, stumbling out of the hut and searching for healthy flesh to corrupt.

The creatures that were born from the giant demon's flesh were all dead now. Each one dissolving on the forest floor. But the village was alive with movement. Each of the villagers now shambling around, vomiting and hacking. They all moaned, barely able to walk without falling over. Their skin had become a dark green color, seeping more green fluid as the flesh started to break open and slough off their bones.

They came for the chief, all of them, reaching for him with slimy fingers. The chief turned to run, now sure that the fire god had turned His back on them, had dropped this hell on them to eradicate the village. Kill them all. But when the chief spun away from the dripping, diseased horde that was his tribe only moments before, he was face to face with the red demon, its fiery eye glaring down at him like the sun.

The monster was no longer weeping. It sat up straight, now ignoring the chief, and sniffed the air. Saliva poured from its mouth. The rumble thundering from its stomach quaked the ground.

The demon stood, licked its lips, and then rushed toward the center of the village, stepping directly over the chief and straight for the tribe.

The sick villagers flocked toward the creature as it devoured them by the handfuls, as if they couldn't wait to be eaten alive. Green slime gushed from the monster's mouth as it stuffed the diseased bodies into it.

The chief hid behind a tree. Watched in horror and disgust as his people, or what used to be his people, willfully gave themselves to the red demon.

Then the wooden trunks nearly bent in half as the wind picked up. The air became so hot, it was hard for the chief to breathe. Sweat spewed from his pores, and he leaned up against the tree, fighting back the tears.

He had done nothing but try and please the fire god. He had taught his people to worship Him, to sacrifice their own children to Him.

The wind continued to grow strength, and then a roar exploded from the sky. The fire god appeared, blocking out the sun with its mass.

A stream of fire exploded from the fire god's mouth as it circled the village, burning the trees, the huts. The chief left his staff behind, ran as fast as his body would allow him into the center of the massacre. He raised both fists into the air and cursed the fire god for betraying him and his people.

A wall of fire swallowed him whole, along with all the trees around him. He only had time to scream once before the fire god's jaws snapped shut over his body and silenced him forever.

A LATE BLOOMER

Krick couldn't stop eating. The smell turned him ravenous—all that succulent, diseased flesh—and he sat cross-legged in the middle of the now-burning village as the sick humans climbed over each other to offer themselves to him. At first, he had wanted to stop his minions from hurting the people, from making them sick. But as soon as that smell hit him, all he could think about was eating. And this meat was…incredible. Nothing like the meat he had force-fed himself before.

If I knew humans could taste like this…I would have been killing them a long time ago.

He thought about what his mother had told him. That humans are food for monsters, just as goats and chickens are food for humans. There's nothing wrong with eating them, he told himself as the green and red gore dripped from his mouth. This is who I am. This is who I was always supposed to be. Besides, they attacked me first.

Handful after handful, he crammed his mouth, chewed, swallowed, went back for more. The dissolving carcasses of his miniature minions lay all around him.

It was like he was in a trance now, gorging himself, possessed by his voracious appetite.

Something heavy landed behind him, and he knew he should probably face it, but he didn't care. Only filling his belly mattered. He growled, hissed, hoping that whatever was behind him would heed his warning and leave him be.

"What…what did you do?"

The voice sounded familiar, but Krick only growled again, slammed the last of the villagers into his mouth and crushed the contaminated flesh with his teeth, basting his tongue in the spicy juices.

"I've never seen anything like that…why didn't you do that before? If your father—"

"M-my father?" Krick swallowed the masticated meat, stood, curled his hands into fists as hard as boulders. As he pictured his father in his mind, heard his father's voice talking about killing him, disowning him, something in his head started to swell, expand. It felt like an open fire inside of his brain, and he snarled, spun toward the voice behind him. "My father can burn in hell!"

An orange and red pillar of fire exploded from Krick's eye, narrowly missing Tyranogon who had to dive out of the way. The fire burned a hole right through the trees behind his grandfather, the entire forest now aflame.

Krick took a deep breath, calmed the pressure in his brain. He wiped the tears from his eye, gasped as Tyranogon struggled to rise back to his feet. Krick ran to him, hands out in front of him.

"I'm so sorry! I didn't-I didn't realize that was you. I

kind of…lost myself there. Tyranogon…I'm really really sorry. Please don't—"

"Grandpa. Call me Grandpa." Tyranogon stared at Krick with a wide, toothy grin on his face.

Krick reached up, touched his eye. Did that fire really come out of me? Was that my special ability?

Krick only wished that his brother and sister could have seen him. They would have shit themselves for sure. And his father. His father might finally be proud of him, might finally accept him into the family.

Krick couldn't help but smile, wanted to jump up and down and shout with joy, but held back, kept cool in front of his grandfather.

"I'll be honest," Tyranogon said. "I thought the villagers were going to kill you. I was kind of counting on it, you know? I was going to tell your mother that there was an accident while I was trying to train you. But clearly…I was wrong about you. Everyone is wrong about you."

Krick was nearly offended that his grandfather was trying to have him killed, but he was still too excited about this special ability to care.

"I thought you didn't like to kill people. You looked pretty pleased if you ask me," Tryanogon said, spitting fire into the air as he laughed and pointed to the burning village.

Krick wiped the mess from his mouth, smacked his lips. "I didn't mean to eat them all. But I was hungry… and they smelled so good!"

He looked back toward the village, his minions

now reduced to bubbling puddles of liquid sizzling in the fire. The village and trees around them crackled as they burned, the air full of black smoke. Krick did feel bad for killing them all, but he couldn't deny that it felt right. Like this is what he was supposed to do.

A late bloomer, that's what Mom said. Maybe she was right. Maybe I finally bloomed!

Tyranogon poked a claw at one of Krick's spots. "Those tiny things that come out of you. What are they?"

Krick shrugged. "Don't know. It just happens sometimes. Whenever I get scared, I think. Any time I feel threatened. There's never been more than a few at a time before, though. I was always embarrassed. My dad said it was a useless, stupid ability. And I believed him…"

Tyranogon just stared at Krick, eyes wide, slightly shaking his head. But it wasn't disappointment in his eyes. Krick was used to seeing that. Tyranogon looked… excited.

Krick put his hands behind his back, rocked back and forth on his feet. "So…what just happened?"

Tyranogon chuckled, flicked his tongue. "What just happened is…I think we may have found the key to destroying Eternal City."

"Wait…what are you—"

Tyranogon stared up at the sky, smiling, the flames dancing around him and casting their orange light over his black scales. "Krick, you just might be the most ferocious monster I've ever seen. Even more so than myself. Now come on!"

Before Krick could say another word, his grandfather's

claws seized him by the shoulders and they were flying through the air, back toward the volcanoes.

MONTAGE

His grandfather's words repeated themselves in his mind, again and again. How can I be the most ferocious monster in the world? That doesn't make any sense.

Tyranogon had been busy for hours, shaping the molten rock into tall, building-like structures. Krick just sat there, trying to will his minions to pop out of him again. No matter how hard he tried, how hard he concentrated, he could only force out one at a time.

Concentrating on his eye now, he pushed and pushed until he gave himself a headache, but no pillar of fire. Not even a wisp of smoke. He would have thought he had imagined the entire incident if his grandfather hadn't been there to witness it.

"Grandpa?"

"Uh-huh." Tyranogon was making some finishing touches to the cooling rock, stood back and admired his work. It really did look like some kind of stone city.

"How can I destroy Eternal City? I can't even control my abilities. They'll kill me!"

Tyranogon shook his head. "They'll never see you coming, Krick. They're expecting some giant Kaiju. Like myself. They've prepared for it, perfected their defense. Even at my prime, I failed. But you? You're special. You'll get under their skin, destroy them from the inside out."

"But…how?"

Tyranogon opened his wings, stretched them as far as they would go. Lava spilled from his mouth like a waterfall as he stomped toward Krick, eyes now wide with rage. He tilted his head back and roared, so loud that he dwarfed the sound of the volcanic eruptions all around them.

Krick jumped to his feet, searched around them to figure out what it was that had upset his grandfather so suddenly. But they were alone.

Tyranogon shot a massive wall of flame toward Krick, completely surrounding him with fire. The giant Kaiju's hand came crashing down at Krick, barely missing him, crushing the rock where Krick had been sitting.

Krick covered himself, couldn't stop his body from shaking. Whatever semblance of courage he had built up had just been swallowed by Tyranogon's roar.

And then they came. Pushing out of his spots. The minions fluttered toward Tyranogon, but were quickly killed by the heat, uselessly plopping to the ground and melting at once.

And then Tyranogon's roar became raucous laughter, and he slapped his belly as he spat flames into the air with each chuckle. He dropped down to his knees and scooped up a few of the liquefying bodies.

"These minions of yours, Krick. They are the key. This is why you were brought to me, don't you see? It's fate. Together we can take that city down. Show the world that nothing can save them from the monsters."

Krick smiled, picked up one of the minions and studied it in his palm. "Like the people in that village."

"Exactly. This is where all of the others have failed at destroying Eternal City. They concentrate on stopping the weapons. Destroying the buildings. It's the people, Krick. The humans. We get down there with them, destroy them on their level. The rest will follow naturally." The minions in his hand had dissolved to liquid, and he wiped it off, patted Krick on the head. "Your minions will spread the disease, and the people will flock to you, rendering their weapons useless. The buildings…the entire city will be ours for the taking!"

Krick wanted to be excited, but there was still something about Eternal City that couldn't be stopped by tiny disease-spreading minions. "Um…Grandpa? What about the Hero? How am I supposed to—"

"The Hero," Tyranogon said, slamming his fist into the side of the volcano. "That's what this is for." He pointed to the rock structures he had just made. "Now get up, Krick. We need to figure out how to control that fire burning inside of you."

"I can't. I've been trying," Krick said as he stood beside his grandfather. "It just shot out of me on its own. I can't control it."

"You will. You see these?" Tyranogon said, wrapping his arm around Krick's shoulders. "I want you to imagine these are buildings. The humans have their weapons locked and loaded and pointed right at your face. Destroy or be destroyed. Go!"

Tyranogon shoved Krick in the back with his massive knuckle. The blow sent Krick flying forward, his feet leaving the ground as he spun through the air, finally slamming into one of the stone pillars. Krick landed on his head, his feet hanging over his face. He smiled at his grandfather as stone debris rattled down around him. Tyranogon ran his scaly palm across his face and shook his head.

"We've got some serious work to do," he said. "Now get up. On your feet! Get angry!"

"Angry," Krick said as he rolled back to his feet and dusted himself off. "Okay, yeah. Angry."

"Ready?"

"Ready!" Krick gave a thumbs up, then balled up his fists and faced the mock city. He bared his teeth, tried to picture his brother and sister, tried to picture the little girl he failed to save. A growl rattled from his throat as he bared his teeth, and then he launched himself forward.

Krick lowered his shoulder as he rushed the first pillar. But rather than smash through it, his spongy body bounced off of it, sent him cartwheeling into the next one where he ricocheted off again. His body was like a pinball as it bounced from pillar to pillar, and he grunted with each impact, growing dizzy as he spun and rolled through the air. He hit the final column, breaking the stone in half. He landed in the ash on his back, and could only watch as the top half of the stone building crashed down on top of him.

Krick groaned as he dug himself out of the rubble,

wincing at the sharp pain in his back. He climbed back to his feet, studied the broken pillar for a second, then turned to Tyranogon who still stood in the same spot as before, lava dripping from his jaws.

"How was that?" Krick said.

The villagers just stared up at Krick, none of them seeming to know what to make of him.

Krick wanted to roar at them, shake the ground with his stomping feet and make them run in terror, but he didn't know where to start. It felt awkward, unnatural. He looked skyward, hoping to find Tyranogon soaring overhead. If he could just give Krick a head start, get these men and women with white paint spread across their faces to run and panic, Krick thought he could take it from there.

But one glance toward the sky revealed that he was alone.

When he swung his head back down to face the tribe again, they all flinched, some of their spears shaking in their fists.

Hey, look at that. They are scared of me after all. I'll give them something to really be scared of.

Krick squeezed his eye shut, tensed his muscles, and pushed. He concentrated on his spots, tried to visualize his minions squeezing out, birthing from his flesh. And then he felt it. That tingling feeling.

I did it! he thought as his eye burst open.

The villagers had their weapons lowered, some of

them tilting their heads as they watched the one minion flutter down from Krick's body toward the forest floor.

"Shit! Shitshitshit!" Krick slammed his foot down, squashing the minion to paste beneath his foot.

The tribe flinched again, then charged toward Krick, all screaming and raising their weapons high. Spears whooshed through the air, the pointed tips plunging into Krick's flesh. They stung, but Krick tried to stand his ground, picking the splinters out of his skin and growling at the approaching horde.

But that did nothing to slow them, and they surrounded him, stabbed at him and beat him and cut him. Before long, Krick was balled up again, his usual defensive tactic, crying as the spear tips entered him from every angle.

Tingling. So intense and sudden that it tickled, turned Krick's weeping into giggling. The minions flowed from his spots and descended down on top of the villagers. The men and women fought them at first, but it didn't take long before they were covered in green, juicy disease and running back to their huts where they began to attack each other.

Krick's stomach rumbled and he sniffed the air. Drool flowed past his nubby teeth and splashed over the ground, and he reached out to the newly infected humans and pulled them toward him, ready to fill his belly with spicy sickness. And they obeyed, shoving one another as they came as if fighting for who got to be eaten first.

A strong wind exploded from above, and Tyranogon slammed to the earth. He folded in his wings and held out his massive hands. "Wait, Krick."

"I'm starving. I did good, right? See? Now it's time to eat."

"You control them."

"I can't control them. I tried. They just come out when I'm in trouble, all on their own."

"The humans, Krick. Once the infection is in them, they are yours."

It was true. The minions seemed to have a mind of their own, but once they spread their disease into the humans, Krick could feel them immediately in his mind. Like they became a part of him, and extension of him.

But right now, Krick only wanted to eat. He wanted to eat so bad.

"Tell them to go the other way. There's another village just past those trees there. A sister village, allies to these people. Tell them to infect them, all of them."

Krick growled, could feel the heat building up in his eye. "No. Hungry!"

"Do it!" Tyranogon roared, spitting fire and lava across Krick's body.

The heat in his eye now extinguished, Krick nodded, reached out to the villagers and instructed them just as Tyranogon said.

The tribe halted immediately, green bile dripping from their faces. As a horde, they turned the opposite direction and began trudging through the forest, past their huts, and into the trees.

"Wait for it," Tyranogon said, now grinning. His head was tilted as he listened.

Krick didn't have to hear it to know. He could feel it. The infected had reached the other village and were spreading the sickness. The screams and shouts of the healthy blasted into the air and scared birds from their nests.

"That a boy! You did it, Krick! You did it!" Tyranogon slapped Krick on the back, and though the blow sent tremors of pain down Krick's spine, he managed to smile up at his grandfather.

"Can we eat now?"

"Sure. Just tell them all to march back here, all of them, and you can feast until you've got humans coming out of your ears."

In a few moments, the now larger horde paraded across the forest toward them, splashing slime across the foliage as they gurgled and vomited.

Tyranogon clapped and cackled as he watched them come.

"Fantastic, Krick. Fan fucking tastic. Let's eat."

"I can't," Krick said, spitting blood from his mouth. He wiped the sweat from his brow as he climbed back to his feet. His body ached, bruised and battered. He averted his eye, which was swollen almost shut, so he didn't have to look his grandfather in the face. "How can I be the fiercest monster if I can't even destroy a building? I'm not strong enough…"

Tyranogon spat two balls of flame from his nostrils as he scratched his chin. "Destroying buildings isn't important, kid. Any monster can do that. Forget about physical strength. Focus on the inferno burning inside of you. I know you can feel it."

"Grandpa…" Krick fought back the tears. He tried to look deep inside himself, feel the heat, but there was only sadness and disappointment boiling within. "Maybe my dad is right. I'm just a—"

"A failure? An embarrassment to the family?"

Krick nodded.

"You want to talk about an embarrassment…look at me, Krick. When I was younger, I was unstoppable. I crushed cities in my sleep. Adult humans would tell stories to their children about me, teaching them to fear me, filling their heads with nightmares. I was a god. And then…" Small wisps of smoke drifted from the corners of his eyes.

"I didn't know I was related to you until my mother dropped me here. My brother and sister still don't. But we all look up to you. You're like a superhero."

"Monster. Don't say the H word."

"Right, sorry. Supermonster, then. My brother used to pretend to be you when he beat me up. Nobody ever saw you as a failure. Every monster who ever tried to take down Eternal City died. All of them except you."

"Maybe I should have died. I still failed. The city still stands. The Hero still lives."

"But you almost destroyed it. You almost defeated the Hero. Nobody sees you as a failure, Grandpa. You are still the most legendary monster ever. I can't believe I'm…related to you." And then he felt it. It started in his gut, bubbling like the magma in the volcanoes. It rose up his body, into his head until he thought he would explode. The heat swelled and filled his eye socket.

Krick's mind raced as the heat intensified. He saw the look of disappointment and shame on his father's face, the sneers and mocking grins of his siblings. He relived all the times his mother had to protect him, all the times his brother and sister made fun of him or beat him up. He heard his father's voice again as he disowned Krick, threatened to kill and eat him.

I'm not a failure. I'm not a disappointment. I'm the fiercest motherfucking monster in the world!

I'm Tyranogon's blood!

"Rrrraaaaaaahhhhhhhh!"

A massive beam of fire exploded from his eye, blasting through the stone pillars and turning them to rubble and smoking ash. The inferno rocketed forward, burning its way through a volcano in the distance. Lava sprayed into the air as the mountain was destroyed. Trees burned on the horizon.

When the blast finally ceased, Krick collapsed backward onto his rump. He gasped for breath as he gawked at the destruction he had caused. Flakes of ash and glowing cinders rained down all around him, and he jumped to his feet and cackled, pumping his fists.

"I did it! Did you see? I did it!"

Tyranogon was on the ground, using his arms and wings to shield his head. One of his great black eyes poked out and landed on Krick, then he unfolded himself and rose back to his feet.

"You almost blew a hole through me," he said, smoke puffing from his mouth with every word. He turned and faced the devastation his grandson had just caused, stayed that way for long enough that Krick wondered if he had done something wrong.

"I'm sorry, Grandpa. I didn't meant to—"

"Look at that. Look at that!" Tyranogon flapped his wings, lifted into the air, then slammed back to the ground just behind Krick. "Again. Do it again."

Krick feared that he wouldn't be able to, that it would be just like before. Like the fire had a mind of its own, just like the minions. But he could still feel it boiling inside of him. He gathered all of his anger and sadness and angst until the pressure built, until his body shook, and then released.

The fiery pillar ripped through the air, obliterating another volcano and sending lava splashing across the scorched earth.

Tyranogon cheered and breathed a massive ball of flame into the clouds. Krick smiled so hard his cheeks hurt, and he turned and beamed up at his grandfather.

"One day," Tyranogon said as he lifted Krick into his arms and flapped his wings until they hovered over the volcanic valley, "they'll tell stories about you, Krick. The monster who destroyed the indestructible city. The descendent of the great and powerful, and motherfucking legendary, Tyranogon!"

"Really? You really think so?"

Tyranogon flapped his wings harder, and they soared higher. A mighty roar exploded from his mouth as he shot another celebratory firestorm into the sky.

Krick widened his eye and unleashed another blast that cut through Tyranogon's flame and shot toward the blazing sun.

Tyranogon laughed, stretching his great wings as they soared over the forest. Krick climbed out of his grandfather's hands, gripping the black scales as he crawled up the neck and finally planted himself on top of Tyranogon's head. He wrapped his fingers around the horns there and howled as they cut the sky.

Tyranogon sprayed the trees with more flame, whooping as the foliage blazed. Krick joined him, unable to stop smiling as the optical heat eradicated trees and scurrying animals below. They flew for miles, burning patterns into the earth beneath them, grandfather and grandson.

"You want to see something, Krick?" Tyranogon said as they coasted through the clouds.

"What is it?"

"Hold on. Haven't done this in a long time."

"What are you—"

"Hold tight!"

Tyranogon tucked his wings and spun his body through the air. He shot fire and lava from his mouth, the flame and glowing magma spiraling around them as they drilled through the sky. Krick screamed, digging his claws into Tyranogon's hide, sure he was going to lose his grip and go flying off into oblivion.

And then the sky seemed to open up as if the heat burned a hole right through it. A crackling void filled with the darkest black Krick had ever seen. They sped toward it, Krick now shutting his eye and shrieking.

One second there was fierce wind, and then nothing. No wind, no sound, no anything. They floated through the nothing in slow motion. And then the nothing opened up, exploded back into reality as wind and color and heat engulfed them once again.

Krick didn't realize he was still screaming until the nothing closed back up behind them and the sound of his shrieking returned.

"Still got it!" Tyranogon said, then flapped his wings again, flying them toward a chain of snow-topped mountains. He perched on top of the tallest peak and folded his wings. "Still with me?"

Krick's fingers ached as he released his death grip on Tyranogon's scales. His chest heaved as he tried to catch his breath, still sitting on top of his grandfather's head. A heavy fog lay across the sky like smoke drifting off smoldering wreckage, but Krick could see shapes on the other side of it, and when he squinted, he could tell it was a city.

"What just happened?" Krick said once he got his breathing back under control. He could still feel the nothing inside of him as if his body had absorbed it as they passed through the void, and his flesh throbbed as if pushing it back out. "Where are we?"

"We teleported. One of my many abilities. To be honest, it's been so goddamn long since I tried that, I wasn't sure I could still do it. Good thing we made it through, too. Don't want to get stuck in the darkness. I know Kaiju who went in and never came back out again."

"You mean…we could have died in the…darkness?"

"Not sure I'd call it dying, but we would cease to exist. But I had confidence. First time in a long time since I could say that. And it's all thanks to you, Krick."

Krick wanted to be upset that Tyranogon had been so careless with their lives, but he couldn't. The only thing he could do was smile.

"You see that there, past the fog?"

"The city?"

"Not just any city."

"Is that…?"

Tyranogon didn't have to answer. He blew a wave of flame into the air and roared. Lava flowed from his mouth and ran down the mountain, melting the ice and causing an avalanche that boomed like thunder as it rolled down.

"We're not going over there, are we?" Krick's bravery began to slip away, rolling down the hill along with the melting ice and snow.

"No. Not yet. Your abilities are powerful. But you still need to get in touch with your inner monster. With the universal Kaiju consciousness."

Krick didn't know what any of that meant, but he trusted Tyranogon. He wanted to make his grandfather proud, wanted to make his whole family proud. He wanted to make other Kaiju look up to him the way they looked up to Tyranogon.

"It's almost time, Krick. Soon, we'll make monster history. Soon, you become a legend."

***

Krick and Tyranogon stood at the top of neighboring volcanoes, the glowing magma spraying from the mountain's blowhole, beading up and sliding off their bodies.

Krick cracked his eye open and peeked at his grandfather who balanced on one leg. His wings were spread out wide, arms posed rigidly in front of him. Wisps of smoke curled out of his nostrils and between his teeth. His scales reflected the bright orange light of the heat.

Waves of acidic euphoria spread through Krick's core as he closed his eye again and refocused. The darkness behind his lid started to swirl and spin. Shapeless blobs of darker black bobbed at the edges of his veiled vision. Sparkles of color began to form, twinkling like stars, and as he tried to focus on them, they would expand and wrap themselves around his being. And they showed him things. It was as if he was looking through the eyes of monsters past, experiencing the destruction of now pulverized cities. He could feel the stone and metal and glass crushing in his fist and beneath his feet; could smell the smoke and blood and cooking flesh; could taste the humans as his teeth ground them up and his tongue was bathed in blood and entrails; could feel the pain and agony as each of these monsters was defeated by the humans' weaponry. As Krick flowed through these visions, the various cities all became one.

Monster after monster fell in Eternal City, some being obliterated by missiles and bullets and fire. But most were slain by the Hero, staring up at his metallic face as the last shred of life drifted away. Krick felt their pain, their shame, their disappointment, and their fear. When Krick opened his eye, now swimming in tears, the only emotion left was anger. Viscous, bubbling anger burning hotter than the lava beneath him. A deep growl crackled from his throat. Minions poured from his skin in a constant flow, each of them dying almost instantly. He bellowed and unleashed an optic heat blast into the air, then dropped to his knees, gasping and weeping. A strong hand grabbed hold of his shoulder and squeezed.

"You felt them."

"All of those monsters. So many…"

"You're ready, Krick. You're ready to avenge them all."

Tyranogon sat atop the nearest volcano, doing sit-ups and grunting. He had slimmed down considerably since he began training with Krick, and was starting to look more like his old self.

Krick faced the valley of volcanoes. The inferno rose from his gut to his head, and he held it there, letting it build. He released a small blast that destroyed the closest mountain, then cut it off, turned, and let loose with another controlled shot. He laughed as he destroyed a tall volcano in the distance, his aim perfect, and then wiped the scalding tears from his eye.

I can't wait to see the looks on everyone's faces when they see me now. How about now, Dad? Huh? Am I still a fucking embarrassment?

When the smoke cleared and the throbbing in his

head had eased, images of the now deceased monsters spun through his mind, and he cringed from the pain in his skull, clenched his teeth as he imagined blasting a hole through the Hero's chest.

Mom was right. We are monsters. Monsters are supposed to destroy. This is who I really am.

A screech rang out in the distance.

Mom?

Condoria soared over the volcanoes, flapping her wings excitedly. Something dangled from her talons. Something huge, weighing her down.

Oh God…Dad?

The giant ice monster held onto Condoria's legs as she flew. The sky thickened with a dense fog as the snow began to fall. Lava became rock instantly, clogging up the volcanoes as Avalanx dropped from the sky and landed just in front of Krick, creating a massive ice-filled crater.

Krick backed away from him, his head thumping again.

Mom landed, and that's when Krick noticed that Gigataur and Zapstress had been riding on her back. They hopped off their mother and faced Krick.

They're here to kill me. I won't let them. His father took a step toward him, hands out as if in surrender. Before he could mutter an icy word, Krick's eye erupted with fire, narrowly missing his father's head. "Krick! Krick, stop!" His mother's voice.

Krick spun on his heels, faced his mother and siblings. "You betrayed me, Mom. You brought them here…but it's different now. I won't let them push me around anymore!"

Another powerful blast exploded from his eye, hitting Gigataur in the middle of his chest and throwing him across the land. He smashed into a volcano, grunted, then fell to the ground, kicking his legs and whimpering.

"Krick...you've got it all wrong!" Mom sped toward him, held him close. "Baby...we're not here to kill you. Your father...your father has something he wants to say."

"W-what?" Krick took long, deep breaths to calm the pounding in his skull. He turned to face Avalanx who had built an ice dome around himself for protection.

Two giant hands burst free from the frozen dome, and the face that emerged was devoid of any rage. It was an expression that Krick had never seen on his father's face. Not toward him at least.

"Krick..." his father started, then shot Condoria a look that said 'Do I have to?'

Condoria squinted at him, nodded, nudged Krick toward him.

"I'm sorry," Avalanx said. "You know...about threatening to kill you and everything. It's just... Look. I was wrong. Dead wrong about you, son." He dropped to his knees, icicles falling from his eyes and shattering on the ground. "We saw you. We saw what you did to those villages. All of us. Right, kids?"

Zapstress nodded, forced a smile when Krick locked his eye with hers. A sheen of electric power flowed over her.

Gigataur brushed himself off, limped toward Krick. The armored plates on his chest and stomach were black, smoking, a couple of them cracked and leaking blood. But when he reached his brother, he put his arm around him. "We saw it, Krick. In our minds. Like when Mom and Dad are destroying. I've…I've never seen anything like that. I'm sorry. I'm sorry for everything."

Tyranogon had still been sitting on his volcano, and he launched himself into the air and hovered over the family, letting lava run from his mouth and splatter all around them. He glared at the Kaiju family as if he were ready to attack.

Krick took one look at him and the smile melted off his face. He pulled Gigataur's arm off his shoulder, faced his father again. "It's not over. There's still something I need to do. For Grandpa. For myself. For monsters everywhere."

"Holy shit…is that Tyranogon?" Gigataur stared up at the great beast with his jaw hanging.

"He's kinda pudgy, isn't he?" Zapstress said. "I always pictured he'd be more menacing and less of a fat ass."

Tyranogon's mouth overflowed with lava as he growled at his other two grandchildren. He unleashed a tidal wave of flame at them, and though they both shrieked, neither was harmed.

"Kids…this is Tyranogon. Your grandfather," Condoria said.

"What?" they both said together.

Avalanx ignored Gigataur and Zapstress as they swooned over their grandfather, firing off question after question, jumping up and down like a couple of excited children. He pulled Krick to the side, put his arm around his son for the first time.

Krick tried to remain strong, to show no emotion.

He wanted his father to respect him, and the old Krick, the one who could cry at the drop of a hat, was dead. The new Krick, however, still craved his father's embrace, his acceptance.

"Son…you have no reason to forgive me. I've been a terrible father. But I can admit when I'm wrong. You are my son, my blood. You proved to me that you are a real monster. Please…let's go home. Destroy cities together. As a family."

Krick pushed Avalanx away, puffed out his chest. "There's something I have to do, Dad. A city I have to destroy. Just like you always wanted. Just like you've been telling me since the day I was born."

"Krick, I was—"

"Right. You were right, Dad. I'm a monster. I destroy. I kill. I eat humans. I understand that now."

"Then let's go home. All of us. What city do you need to destroy that's more important than your—"

"Eternal City."

Everyone went quiet then. Avalanx flinched, squinted at his son, then shot a look at Condoria. Her beak hung open, feathers falling from her body and fluttering to the icy, ash-covered ground. Gigataur and Zapstress peeled their attention away from their idol to gawk at their little brother.

Condoria shook her head, hopped into the air and landed beside Krick. She tried to wrap him in her wing, but he pushed her away. "Krick. What…why would you want…?" Then her eyes slowly turned toward Tyrano-gon. "Dad? Did you put this idea in his head? Fucking

Eternal City? Are you insane?"

Tyranogon snorted twin fireballs. "He can win. He can destroy Eternal City. I know he can."

"You son of a bitch!" Avalanx opened his mouth, exhaled an ice beam at the old Kaiju, but Tyranogon countered with his own blast of hellfire. The abilities canceled each other out in midair and filled the sky with steam.

The two Kaiju men roared at each other, the ground shaking and the wind blasting as they closed the distance between them. Even Condoria looked ready to attack Tyranogon, while Gigataur and Zapstress just watched, dumbfounded.

"Enough!" Krick's head pulsed, but he was able to hold back the heat.

His family hushed at once, all eyes on him.

"Dad, just the other day, you said you wanted to kill me. Eat me or let Gigataur and Zapstress do it for you."

"Krick, I—"

"Shut up and let the boy talk, Aval. Goddamnit, you—"

"Mom," Krick said, turning to face her. "You flew me here so my grandfather could teach me to be a real monster. You say it's because you were trying to save me…but I saw the way you couldn't even look at me after Pelican Bay. You were embarrassed too."

Condoria hung her head.

"Gigataur…Zapstress. I think you both know you've done nothing but make my life hell. Always making fun of me, always making me feel worthless. Now what? You see me destroy a couple of villages and you want to be friends now? You don't want to kill me anymore?"

Neither of his siblings had anything to say. Krick couldn't believe he was standing up to his family like this. Part of him believed that he would never survive Eternal City. That this was his last chance to tell them how he really felt before he was killed.

But I have to do this. I can feel it.

"Mom, Grandpa's right. I can do this. He might have put the idea in my head, but it's my decision. I have to go to Eternal City. I have to prove to myself that I can do it. That I'm a real monster. A Kaiju."

Condoria kept her head down, tears splashing to the ground at her feet. Feathers continued to fall away from her body. Gigataur and Zapstress now looked at Krick the way they had looked at Tyranogon—with admiration. Just to see that look in their eyes made Krick feel invincible.

"Let us come with you," Zapstress said. "The three of us. We'll smash that fucking city. Rip that giant hero's balls off and hang them from the tallest building."

"Fuck yeah," Gigataur said, still grimacing and rubbing his injured torso. "Come on, Krick. It'll be fun."

"No. I'm doing this alone. It's the only way." Krick patted Tyranogon on the leg and the giant Kaiju nodded at him. "It's time to show these motherfucking humans who rules this planet."

Gigataur and Zapstress both cheered. Gigataur rolled into a ball, shot spikes into the air. Zapstress put on a light show, turning the sky electric blue.

Avalanx just stood there, precipitating sleet from his mouth with every heavy breath. The entire place was nearly covered in snow now.

Condoria finally lifted her head. "Krick, please don't do this. Monsters have been trying forever to destroy Eternal City. It's indestructible. Your grandfather knows this firsthand. You...you're not ready. You've only just discovered your abilities. How can you possibly hope to win? There's only death waiting for you there."

Tyranogon growled. "Connie. He's got something the city's not ready for. You saw it. He can win. I know he can. He can take that fucking city down for good."

"And what about you? The great and powerful Tyranogon? You couldn't destroy that city. How can you send—"

"He's the only chance we got! He's—"

"A child! He's a child who is getting in way over his head. And it's your fucking fault!"

Krick patted Tyranogon's leg again. His grandfather swung his head toward Krick, Condoria still screaming and cursing at him.

"Take me there. Now."

Tyranogon nodded, grinned wide as lava poured out from between his teeth. He opened his wings as wide as they would go, flapped them so hard that Krick's family was blown backward. His talons clamped around Krick's arms, lifted him.

Fire and wind and lava and spinning.

Krick could still hear his mother's screams, her pleads as he was smothered with heat.

One moment he was surrounded by volcanoes and ice

and his family. And then they plunged into the nothing, the darkness, swam through the deep black until they reached the other side.

Reality washed over them.

"Good luck, Krick," Tyranogon said. They hovered over Eternal City. "Seize your destiny."

The talons released Krick and he plummeted toward Eternal City. The fire inside of him raged as his feet slammed down in the streets.

Within seconds, an alarm sounded. High-pitched and ear-piercing.

Krick grabbed his head, shook it, tilted his head back and roared.

ETERNAL CITY

It had been years since a Kaiju had dared attack Eternal City. The citizens lived in peace, though the streets were becoming too crowded. Everyone flocked to the city, desperately craving to live a life without constant fear. Every time a city was destroyed, the survivors—if there were any—would immediately rush to Eternal City, begging to be let in, pleading for protection.

They let in as many as they could, but the over-population was quickly becoming a problem. Only those who could work were allowed inside. Those who could contribute to keeping Eternal City exactly that—eternal. Free from the threat of destruction. The only city in the entire world that the monsters feared.

"Another fine day," the general said. He sipped his coffee and watched his men. Expressionless, every one of them. Bored. "Look alive, people."

The men and women of the Eternal Military were becoming restless. Only the best resided in Eternal City, and they craved action. They craved bloodshed. The general felt the same way, but had to keep his craving for violence in check. He had even come up with a plan to fake the giant Hero's death so that Kaiju might be lured into launching some kind of attack. Yes, lives would be lost, but it was for the greater good. The citizens needed to be reminded that they were well-protected. That no creature in the world could defeat their armored city. That they were safer within the iron walls of Eternal City than anywhere else on Earth.

But the only way to remind them was to demonstrate. Lay waste to any Kaiju in plain sight of the people, let them see the power that the city possessed. Remind them why the Eternal Military was an unstoppable force. Undefeatable.

"Sir," one man said. He perked up and stared at his monitor with a wide rictus spread across his face. "Unidentified object hovering above the city."

"Show me." The general finished his coffee and rushed toward his soldier.

"Here, sir. Just appeared out of nowhere. Just like—"

"Tyranogon."

A collective gasp in the room. What had been excitement only moments before warped into fear and uncertainty. The only Kaiju to ever challenge them and nearly win. The Kaiju that was supposed to be dead.

"Ready your stations! Let's remind that son of a bitch why he lost the last time! Let's—"

"Sir, there's something else. It's heading right for the—"

The ground rumbled as the thing slammed down in the center of the city, throwing up a mushroom cloud of dust.

All were quiet. All held their breath and watched. The

general squinted at the giant monitor in front of him.

"Get ready!"

The dust cleared. The knot of panic twisting tighter in the general stomach went loose, and he couldn't help but chuckle as he stared at the foolish monster standing dumbfounded in the center of Eternal City.

Thank God for that.

"Look what we got here. You boys and girls ready to play?"

"Yes, sir!" they all said back. Smiles lit faces, some even laughing and joking with each other.

It was a red, spotted, one-eyed beast with the tiny bat wings. The thing was almost adorable, not like the ferocious and nightmarish monsters they had defeated in the past. The general damn near felt sorry for the thing.

The citizens, of course, screamed, ran, panicked. But that's what they do. That was their role in this: fear.

The soldiers sat at their stations, ready to blast this monster a new asshole, shower the citizens in its gore.

"Not yet. Let's see what it does first."

The general wanted to take his time. Enjoy this. To kill the monster instantly would feel anticlimactic. No. They needed to prolong this. Let the citizens panic for a little while. Let them wonder if this was the day that they would die. Let them doubt the absolute power of Eternal City and its weaponry. They had to let the monster do a little damage. It brought the people together. Gave them purpose. Fueled their hate for the Kaiju.

The alarm was sounded. Not to warn. But to assist in striking fear into the hearts of the very people they were protecting. And it worked like a charm. If the sight of the monster wasn't enough, that constant siren did the trick. The streets were alive with people and cars, all scattering this way and that. Chaos flooded the city.

Though this was going to be child's play, the general was happy to have it. There hadn't been an actual real threat since Tyranogon nearly ended them all those years ago, but even as gargantuan and deadly as he was, they still won. Since then, Tyranogon had not shown his face again, and for that they were proud. The monster was assumed dead. They even had a holiday on the anniversary of their victory each year, a reminder of their greatest triumph. The general could admit to himself that he was relieved Tyranogon didn't show, but there was a hint of disappointment. He craved a real fight as much as he feared it.

This new monster put its hands to its head, bared its teeth. The siren wailed, obviously irritating the beast.

They waited. Surely, this creature would go into a blind rage, just like the others, and begin breaking buildings, smashing cars. Scooping people out of the street and stuffing them into its mouth. And that's when they would strike.

But this strange Kaiju just stood there. Clutching its head. It looked down at the screaming people, the cars zooming by and crashing into one another to escape it. And it just stood there.

The soldiers grew restless, impatient. This monster seemed to be waiting for them to make their move. Something they had never experienced before. They couldn't just sit there, doing nothing. The people would wonder what they were waiting for. Might start doubting the competence of their military, the city.

"Fire one missile," the general said. "Just to piss it off. Don't kill it yet."

"Yes, sir."

A hatch opened up on the top of the building closest to the beast. The monster must have noticed it, because it turned, squinted its giant eye at it. The missile launched, hit the monster in the center of its chest.

The soldiers cheered. The general watched.

The monster roared, its eye pinched shut as it stumbled backward right into another building. It clutched its chest, dropped to its knees.

The room went silent as they awaited the monster's counter attack. It would jump to its feet, smash structures, maybe unleash some kind of power. Lasers or fire or ice.

But it never got up off its knees. It curled into a ball…and seemed to be weeping. The first monster Eternal City had seen in years, and it cried when the first missile hit it.

The men didn't know what to do next. Even the people in the streets had stopped running to watch the spectacle.

"Kill the damn thing. This is a waste of time," the general said. What a fucking disappointment.

Just as the men were readying their weapons, the .general put up a hand.

"Wait…what in the hell?"

Something looked to be growing out of the monster's

skin. The black spots covering its red hide pulsated and thrashed. Tiny monsters broke free, floated down into the street.

"What the hell is this? Zoom in!"

The cameras magnified the scene as more and more of the miniature creatures popped out of the larger one, flapped their puny wings and fluttered down. They looked sick, hacking and vomiting. Looked as if they could keel over and die any second.

One of the creatures floated down into the street, right beside a congregation of spectators. The people still just stood there, watching, not sure of how they were supposed to act. The creature wheezed, could barely walk. Then it opened its mouth wide and expelled a stream of green bile that splashed over the faces of the citizens closest to it.

The people shrieked, tried to wipe the sludge off their skin, out of their eyes, spitting it out of their mouths.

The other creatures did the same as the first. They chased down citizens and sprayed them with vomit or coughed into their faces. As each one of them emptied its sickness, they would fall over and die, a lifespan of about a minute and a half.

"Oh Jesus Christ!" The general slammed his fist on his desk.

The soldiers could only stare at their monitors as they watched their citizens turn on one another. Those who had been puked upon were now chasing down the others, dragging them to the ground, spewing green, liquid disease over them. And then those would get up and do the same to others. Again and again and again.

The streets became mayhem once again as the uninfected scattered. They sprinted and screamed and clambered over one another to escape their friends and family and fellow Eternal City citizens who were now walking plagues. Vomit exploded from mouths and nostrils, splashing over flesh and concrete and iron.

More and more of the tiny creatures broke free from the red Kaiju who was still clutching its chest and weeping, rocking itself, seemingly oblivious to the pandemonium around it.

One woman was pushing a stroller, and she raced away from the creatures and the sick, pushing her baby along as fast as possible. One of the creatures fluttered down on top of the stroller. Before the mother could stop it, the thing unleashed a splash of bile into it. The woman shrieked, knocked the creature away who instantly died when it hit the pavement. In the next moment, an ooze-coated baby leapt onto its mother's face, clutching her hair, vomit gushing out from its toothless mouth and filling hers.

The infected began piling into buildings and businesses. Within minutes, slime and vomit splashed over the windows from the inside. Then the newly infected would stagger out into the streets. There was hardly any room for people to run anymore as more and more bodies added to the crowd.

The infection spread in mere minutes, having an instantaneous effect on its host. Turning them into these vomiting zombies on contact. It seemed there were more infected than healthy now, and the number swelled by the second.

"Kill that fucking thing!" the general roared. "Fire, fire, fire! We're losing control here!"

"Sir…we can't. Our weapons can't reach it."

The missile launchers and giant machine guns had been installed at the top of every building in preparation for the massive Kaiju. But this new creature lay in the street, still curled up. The launchers and guns were not designed to aim down.

"The Hero, sir. We need to call the Hero and end this now!"

"No!" the general said. "We can handle this ourselves. Send the troops."

As the citizens ran away from the monster and the diseased, the troops marched toward it. Armored men and women, each equipped with assault rifles or flame-throwers, a few with rocket launchers resting on their shoulders. Tanks rolled across the pavement and crushed the bodies of the infected. Green ooze splashed over the streets.

As the diseased swarmed them, the soldiers pumped them full of bullets, sprayed them with flame. But it did nothing to slow them. They just kept coming and coming, pulling soldiers to the ground, smothering them with puke.

"Goddammit!" The general grabbed the nearest soldier and punched him in the face. "Get those fucking tanks over there and blow a fucking hole through that giant cocksucker!"

The foot-soldiers were overwhelmed and quickly joined the ranks of the infected. As the tanks rolled on, the infected swarmed them and climbed on. They clawed at the metal to get to the healthy bodies inside.

And then the monster stood.

"Now, now, now! Fire the—"

The door flew open, slamming against the wall. The general spun on his heels, pulled out his pistol. A massive horde of the infected swarmed into the room, most of them his own soldiers. The general fired into the crowd, but his bullets were useless. Not a single rocket was fired before the men were pulled from their stations and marinated in hot, green slime.

Hands clutched at the general, clawed at his skin. A stream of bile shot toward his face, and he ducked it just in time. He threw his pistol, leapt toward the giant red button on his desk. The button that would call the Hero, wake it from its slumber.

The general didn't know what would be left for the Hero to save.

Just as his palm slammed down on the button, he was bathed in boiling plague.

THE
HERO

Krick sniffed the air. His belly rumbled. The succulent odor of disease swirled throughout the city, and Krick craved the taste of the infected flesh.

But he could feel them out there. The people he had changed. They chased the rest of the humans, hunting them, ready to spew their virus onto them. Krick wanted to call them over, wanted to eat, but there was no time.

The humans had used some kind of special power on him, hit him in the chest and knocked the wind out of him. He rubbed the spot where they had hit him, winced at its tenderness. It felt like when Gigataur used to hold him down and punch him, not stopping until Krick would start crying.

I hope nobody saw me crying just now. Maybe the old Krick isn't dead after all.

Just as the thought entered his mind, something exploded right beside his head, taking a chunk out of the metal building beside him.

From down the street, a tank rolled toward him, its

gun aimed up and directly at his eye. It fired, and Krick leapt out of the way just in time.

Another tank turned a corner, fired, hit him in the shoulder. Orange blood oozed down his arm, dripped from his elbow. More and more of his minions popped out of him, but their vomit did nothing to the metal tanks.

Everywhere Krick tried to run, he was met by another tank. Some of the sick humans climbed onto them, tried to pry them open, but were only shredding their own fingertips.

And then his head began to thump, temples pulsating.

Krick shrieked, swung his head back and roared when another tank blast hit him in the neck. The pain blinded him. Blood gushed from the wound. He fell backward, slammed the back of his head against the iron building behind him. The tanks surrounded him now, their guns aimed at his head, each one covered with infected humans slamming their juicy flesh against the metal, splashing green fluid all over the place.

The fire erupted from his eye, shot straight into the air. The red and orange pillar roared out with more force than before, so strong and violent that Krick could hardly stand.

Another tank fired its gun, but the blast was swallowed whole by Krick's optical hellfire. The tank was reduced to ash and liquefied metal in seconds. Krick opened his mouth and bellowed as he spun in place, taking out every tank, burning a deep trench in the concrete. Water sprayed from the street, but did nothing to put out the fire.

Krick panted, curling and uncurling his fists as he stared at the destruction he had caused. The sweet, delicious destruction. He nearly started cheering. He was almost convinced that he had won. That he had done something no other monster could ever do…that he had made history.

Then he remembered. Where's the Hero?

The tallest building in the city began to rumble. Steam billowed from the edges, hissing.

Krick called his people to him, reaching out to them with his mind. He needed his strength, and as they rushed toward him from all directions, stumbling over each other to get to him, he reached down, scooped up handfuls of them, and crammed them into his mouth. Their green, creamy centers ruptured between his teeth, and he moaned as he feasted. His head throbbed and begged him to release the pressure.

The sides of the building began unfolding, opening up like a cardboard box. A translucent goo rushed out, oily and iridescent. It flowed through the streets and splashed against buildings. The massive body inside was curled into a fetal position. Its silver skin dripped with fluid.

Krick wiped his mouth, then touched his neck where his wound continued to bleed profusely. He reached out to his people again, seized them with his mind fingers.

Infect the Hero, he told them.

As the humans sprinted across the city toward the Hero, wading through the sparkling goop that had burst from the building, the Hero uncurled itself, stepped out of its iron womb. Its skin was metallic, sparkled in the light, yet still looked fleshy. Its eyes were dark blue, huge compared to the size of its head. It looked, for the most part, human, besides its size. Its body had humanoid proportions, though long blades stuck out from its elbows. Well-defined, bulging muscles covered its torso and limbs. A cock and balls the size of an apartment building dangled from between its thighs, and just as Krick noticed it, a stream of dark yellow urine flowed out, splashed against the side of a building. The piss blast knocked the infected humans backward as if they were hit with a powerful fire hose.

The Hero stretched, opened his mouth wide and yawned, his voice deep and robotic.

Once he had finished relieving himself, the Hero shook his cock, then stared across the city at Krick. Cracked his knuckles. And smiled.

The plagued humans attempted to climb the Hero, but the goo still coating his body proved too slippery, and they couldn't get any further than his ankle. The Hero studied them, seemed amused, then lifted his foot and stomped down. He didn't seem too concerned that these had once been the very people he had been protecting, didn't show a shred of remorse or compassion. Just kept stomping his feet, turning the horde into a dark green paste smeared across the concrete.

Krick's minions poured out of him, but they were useless against the Hero. Once the Hero became bored with crushing the humans, he glared at Krick again. He struck a martial arts pose and made his eyes light up brighter.

The fire exploded from Krick's eye, sliced buildings in half.

The Hero leapt into the air just in time, kicked off a building and launched himself even higher. He flipped above Krick and let loose with a robotic shriek.

Krick tried to swing his eye upward, but wasn't nearly quick enough. The Hero's foot slammed into the top of his head and sent him tumbling into the closest building, turning it to rubble underneath him and knocking the wind out of him.

Krick moaned, kicked his legs as he tried to catch his breath. Something jabbed him in the side, and though he couldn't tell what it was, he could feel the blood trickling out. The wound on his neck widened and gushed with more blood.

The Hero grabbed Krick by the head, yanked him out of the rubble.

Krick widened his eye, blasted the Hero in the chest and stomach with a fiery optic blast.

The Hero gasped, dropped to a knee as he clutched at the blackened spot on his torso. He bared his silver teeth, spun and hit Krick with a sweep kick. Krick found himself on his back again, his fire shooting uselessly into the sky. What remained of his diseased humans still attempted to crawl up the Hero's body, but kept failing, splattering across the pavement.

The Hero just stood there, motioning for Krick to stand with a flick of his fingers.

Krick didn't want to. This was a mistake, he thought. He's going to kill me.

The Hero kicked Krick in the side, then grabbed him by the fat of his chest and hauled him to his feet. Krick wavered, nearly fell right back down.

My family is watching. I can't fail them again!

Krick bared his teeth, roared. He let loose with another pillar of fire, but the Hero dodged it easily. He did a backflip, landed in a handstand at the top of a building, then launched himself into the air. He rocketed down with his razor-edged elbow.

Krick saw the blade speeding toward his face, and he rolled out of the way just in time. The Hero's elbow blade plunged into a skyscraper, slicing its way through countless floors. When the Hero tried to pull it out, it seemed stuck, and he quickly turned his head toward Krick. Panic ignited in his huge, blue eyes.

Krick didn't waste any time. Still on his back, he hit the Hero in the stomach with his most powerful blast yet. The Hero screamed and tugged on his arm to get it free. Krick lowered his gaze, incinerating his enemy's cock and balls, charring the gigantic genitals until they melted off. Strings of black and red gore stretched from the groin down to the pile of meat smoking in the street.

The Hero bared his teeth and groaned. He pressed his foot up against the building and finally ripped his elbow blade free.

Krick tried to aim for his head, but the Hero flipped out of the way, splashing blood across the skyscraper's side. Krick's beam demolished another building instead. The Hero hopped from building to building, black and red fluid spraying from his mauled groin.

Running through the streets to keep up with the Hero, Krick tried to blast him out of the sky, but kept missing. The Hero was too quick, too agile. The horde of diseased humans followed—they changed direction like a school of fish every time Krick did.

Then he lost him.

What the fuck? Krick thought. Where the hell—

A whistle from behind him. A playful tune. Krick spun on his heels to face it and was met with a massive chunk of rubble. It hit him in the eye, threw him backward off his feet. He rubbed at the throbbing wound, trying to rid it of the debris that burned and scraped against his pupil. When he was finally able to open his eye again, he saw the Hero flying down at him, elbow out, blood trickling from between his legs.

The blade came down on Krick's arm and severed it at the shoulder. It flopped beside him, spurting blood. Krick screamed, tried to use his remaining arm to clutch at the bleeding stump, but the Hero's foot came down on his wrist and pinned it to the street.

Minions flowed from Krick's body, uselessly fluttering to the street and dying. Krick tried to release another torrent of flame at his foe, but the Hero swung down, punched Krick so hard he nearly lost consciousness. Then he hit him again and again and again. Krick's teeth were knocked loose. His mouth was filled with tooth fragments and blood.

The Hero knelt down, put his mouth right up against Krick's ear. "I will destroy all monsters. None of you can stop me. Eternal City will live forever. Motherfucker."

The Hero's eyes ignited with bright light, particles of energy swirling in front of them, building and building, growing larger and brighter, spinning faster and faster.

Krick closed his eye, turned his head, and waited for his death to come.

I'm sorry, Mom. Dad. Grandpa. I failed.

Something soft drifted onto Krick's face. Something cold. He opened his eye just a crack and couldn't help but smile as the snow fell from the sky.

"Get off my son, you dickless cocksucker!"

An icy beam hit the Hero in the chest, threw him backward. A thick block of ice covered his torso, and he frantically bashed it with his fists, breaking it bit by bit as he got back to his feet.

The ground shook, making the Hero stumble. He grabbed the side of the building to keep his balance, but dropped to his knee when four spikes stabbed into his belly and stuck out the other side. Blood rained down, and he gripped the spikes one at a time to yank them out.

Gigataur came rolling out of nowhere, slammed into the Hero, rolled over him and puckered him with more spike wounds. Blood squirted, then rained back down on the Hero like a fountain.

Before he could even sit back up, blue lightning exploded from the sky, engulfed him in voltage that danced and crackled around his body. He seized and foamed at the mouth. The open wound at his crotch smoked and cooked, the blood bubbling.

Zapstress stood on top of a building, the metal underneath her glowing with energy as her electricity wrapped around it. Gigataur uncurled himself, stretched his arms and roared, then smiled at Krick who was just now rising to his feet, clutching at his bleeding stump.

Avalanx pressed his hand to Krick's stump, froze the wound closed. Krick shrieked, but the cold felt good on his wound, and the bleeding stopped. Then Krick's father turned back to the Hero who had risen back to his feet again, though his body was now spewing blood and smoking. Robotic sounds clicked out of his mouth as he gasped and moaned.

Avalanx widened his mouth, eyes bright with icy blue, and unleashed another frozen beam of energy that slammed the Hero against the building behind him. It froze him to the structure so that only his head could move, the rest encased in an icy prison. The Hero's head rolled as he shrieked, cursing the monsters, promising them he would kill each and every one of them.

Two giant shadows passed over them. Krick smiled up at his mother and grandfather as they flapped their wings, settling into the street in front of the Hero. When the Hero locked eyes with Tyranogon, he stopped screaming, eyes widened. Recognition and fear twisted his expression then, and he fought harder than ever to free himself.

"Krick?" Tyranogon said, keeping his eyes on the Hero. "This is your victory. You defeated Eternal City. But please…let me kill this asshole."

The rest of the monsters laughed.

"Be my g-guest, Grandpa," Krick said.

Tyranogon chuckled, stood tall in front of his foe. Lava flowed from his mouth and his eyes glowed red.

Then he opened his jaws wide and spat an inferno into the Hero's face, blasting him until there was nothing left but a black, charcoal nub. Tyranogon reared his head back and roared triumphantly, then swung forward and snapped his jaws over the barbequed head, swallowing it whole.

The family just stood there for a moment, staring at the Hero's decapitated, frozen body. They all gasped, none saying a word. Then they turned toward Krick. And cheered.

"You did it, son," his father said, and picked him up and placed him on his shoulders. "You destroyed Eternal City! You're a goddamn legend!"

The rest of the family danced around Avalanx as he bounced Krick on his shoulders, cackling and sniffling.

Krick forgot about the pain in his arm, the torture pulsating across his body. The rest of the infected humans swarmed the monsters, reaching up to them, begging for them to eat them.

"Let's eat!" Krick said.

The family feasted, complimenting Krick on the zesty flavor of the diseased flesh he had created. Afterward, they patted their bellies, stared at all the buildings still standing in the indestructible city.

"Hey," Krick said. "Let's fuck this place up."

Condoria pecked Krick with kisses, then took to the sky with Tyranogon. She soared over the city, dropping eggs of lava over the streets as Tyranogon cackled and breathed his hellfire down on the standing structures.

Krick, for the first time in his life, joined in on the

destruction with his brother, sister, and father. And together, as a family, they reduced Eternal City into a wasteland.

He had never been happier.